THE MEANEST MAN IN WEST TEXAS

THE MEANEST MAN IN WEST TEXAS

H. B. BROOME

DOUBLEDAY & COMPANY, INC.
GARDEN CITY, NEW YORK
1985

All of the characters in this book
are fictitious, and any resemblance
to actual persons, living or dead,
is purely coincidental.

Library of Congress Cataloging in Publication Data

Broome, H. B.
The meanest man in West Texas.

I. Title.
PS3552.R6598M4 1985 813'.54

ISBN: 0-385-23102-4
Library of Congress Catalog Card Number: 85-1524

Printed in the United States of America

First Edition

For Brookie

THE MEANEST MAN IN WEST TEXAS

CHAPTER 1

I wet my pants just before I shot and killed the second meanest man in West Texas. I was just seventeen and I'll confess that I was green as grass. Like most kids I tried to act older than I was. That's why I was learning how to roll my cigarettes with one hand. Christ, the tobacco I spilled would have filled a barn. Well, anyway, that's the reason—trying to look grown up—that I'd bought an old rusted single-action .44-caliber revolver. You had to cock the son of a bitch to shoot it.

Sometimes it's hard to remember what was real and what wasn't. In a way it's like I'm talking about someone else and not myself. But then my mind can take me back and I can feel the sweat drying on my shirt, and I can smell the horses, and I can see like it was yesterday the darkness inside Malone's place. It was a long, narrow saloon, and it had three kerosene lamps. They hung down and there was a yellow halo around each one that went up on the ceiling. It took a few minutes to adjust your eyes. I was standing inside the door, trying to see, when I heard this voice. It was deep and tough and it said—I'll never forget this—it said, "We don't want no childring in here." That's the way he pronounced it: "childring." I saw the outline of a big man. Of course it was Malone. Everybody knew his reputation. Even I had heard about it and I was brand-new in town. He was standing behind the bar, leaning on it. Then he said, "At first I thought you were a boy but maybe you're a little girl. We don't allow no women or girls or childring in here, so you just get on out."

I was able to see him by then. Things were getting into focus. He was big and had pig-mean eyes. I realize now that he was probably putting on a show for a few of the cowboys in the place. But at the time I was so surprised and frightened that I didn't move, and that seemed to make him mad, really mad. He reached under the bar and pulled out his shotgun and I heard the cowboys get up and walk out. They were wearing spurs that made jingling noises. Malone was crazy and they didn't want any part of him when he got like that. I stood and looked at him as he pointed his shotgun at my belly, and I never felt as weak or as scared before in all my life. That's when it happened. Hell, I didn't even feel it, but he saw the stain on my britches start to spread and get bigger. And he began to laugh. He laughed harder and harder and harder. His eyes filled with tears he laughed so much.

I've never been able to stand being laughed at, and I could feel myself begin to tremble. Rage can shove fear off to one side and that was what was happening.

Malone started coughing and he leaned over the bar in a fit. The click of the hammer being pulled back on my .44 brought his head up just as the pistol went off. Several things happened at once—the explosion inside the bar sounded like a cannon—and Malone jerked backward into the glasses on the shelves behind the bar, and they were crashing as his shotgun roared and blew a hole a foot across in the painted ceiling over my head. It was one of those tin ceilings with square designs on it.

The only thing I could think of was to hide. I was so humiliated about wetting my pants, and I went over to a table where the cowboys had been sitting. There was a bottle and three glasses there. When the people came in I was pouring myself a drink of whiskey. It was the first one I ever had and I was astonished at how raw it tasted.

The men came in real slow, one by one. They looked at me, at the jagged hole in the tin ceiling that was right where a kerosene lamp cast a spot on it, and then they looked over the bar at Jack Malone, the one folks called the second meanest man in West Texas. I heard a fellow say, "He's deader than a doornail." Then they were quiet, looking at me. Due to the condition of my britches I couldn't get up, and I didn't know what to say, so I looked back at them. I heard people talking all at once to each other. Several said, "He's just a kid." One man said, "I was there and I saw him. Malone had his shotgun cocked and pointed at him, and the kid's pistol was holstered. He must be the fastest gun in all of time." And then another voice said, "Well, that may be, but he has a curse. It ain't human to be that cold. He's killed a human being, even if it was Jack Malone, and he's sitting in the dead man's saloon drinking his whiskey." One of the cowboys was talking to a friend saying, "It's like the devil himself crawled inside that young boy." And someone whispered, "Watch yourself. He might hear you."

Then a strange thing happened. I could see the fear take hold of them. They backed out of the door, looking at me. I didn't feel any sense of power. I just felt the wetness between my legs. I poured myself another drink and sat there for a miserable half hour. Then I left. I got on my horse and rode out of town, past the people who were standing all together. I didn't look at them as I passed by. I rode out through the scary darkness to the ranch where I had hired on.

CHAPTER 2

It must have been midnight when I got to the ranch. I unsaddled Bess, my sorrel mare, and broke out a bale of hay for her. While she crunched away on it I scraped the dried lather off her back with the steel curry comb that was in the old shed where we kept our saddles. There weren't any lamps on in the bunkhouse or in the main house either.

The Lower Ranch had been owned by Jason Field for some years, and it wasn't but six miles from town. The Upper Ranch that he owned was twenty miles north, separated from this ranch by the Clarke spread.

I turned Bess out into the horse trap, a pasture where we kept our remuda, then I saw a light come on in the main house. A minute later Mr. Field was standing out by his front porch and I walked up to him.

"Out kind of late, aren't you, son?"

"Yes, sir, I reckon so."

"Well, come on in with me and we'll set a spell. I don't sleep now like I used to."

The big coffeepot was on the back of the black iron stove. There was a smell of wood smoke that hung in the air. The coffee was always there. Every day Mr. Field would throw in more coffee and water and once in a while he would clean it out. Mr. Field lived alone and took most of his meals at the bunkhouse, where we had a cook. But he did keep his coffeepot, and some days he would have his meals sent up to him when he was feeling poorly.

He knew something was wrong though I hadn't said much. We sat there, quiet, and then he said, "You better tell me what's on your mind."

Later, when I had told my story, he said, "I'll try to help. When I was a little older than you I got into a scrape. To tell the truth I was in quite a few." I had heard a few stories and knew that he had been known as a gunfighter long ago, but I didn't say anything.

"You'd best get on to bed, boy. We'll be up working at daylight." He smiled a little and touched me on the shoulder as I left him. That doesn't sound like much, but at the time it happened it meant a lot to me.

In the next few weeks I stayed clear of Santa Rita. There was just no real need to go to town, and I wanted things to blow over and be forgotten. But that wasn't to be. I realized that there was no way I could undo the shooting of Jack Malone. Something that happened in just a few seconds was going to change my life.

Jason Field knew. Hell, it wasn't in him to pretend. One Sunday afternoon he sent for me and when I got to his house he had me sit in a rocker on the porch. I sat there feeling the breeze, looking at the chair, not knowing what to do or say. The rocker had been made on the place out of mesquite wood with the bark still on it. The seat and back were cowhide. The hair on the hide was wearing a little but it was comfortable. Mr. Field had something in his lap, all wrapped up in newspaper, and after a spell he handed it to me, saying, "You'll be needing this, Tom."

It was his old six-gun. It was a Colt .45 and it was in beautiful condition. It was a double-action revolver that didn't have to be cocked to fire. The feeling of balance of that handgun was remarkable. It was in a holster that had been kept oiled, and it was supple and soft in my hands. The belt was full of cartridges and the holster had tie-down leather thongs to go around the right leg. There wasn't any doubt about it, this was a gunfighter's rig.

"It would be a big mistake for most folks to wear this," Jason Field said, and his voice sounded a little sad. "When you put it on it seems to say, 'I'm on the prod, come on and try me.' There's no help for it. You can't walk around the fact that the cocky little bantie roosters who want to make a reputation are going to be out to put a bullet in you. They'll want to have it known that they killed the man who outgunned Jack Malone. Now, I don't know how you done that, but I expect it was with a fair amount of luck."

He stopped for a minute, studying my face, and then, with a grunt, he picked up a good-sized wooden box. "This is full of cartridges. I'm going to send you to the Upper Ranch for the winter. Old Juan has been alone long enough, and you'll relieve him. I'll ride up with you, and then Juan and I will show you what has to be done. When we get there, I'll spend an hour a day with you working on gun handling. I don't want you to be a gunfighter. God knows it took me half a lifetime to live down the name. But I do want you to be able to stay alive. And if you do what I tell you, if you have the coordination and the quickness, you may live to see twenty-one."

I didn't know what to say. I was grateful on the one hand, and I was worried on the other. I was worried about being alone, and about whether I could handle the job of looking after his cattle. And I was scared about what he had been telling me. I was Tom English. I hadn't really lived yet—and I had always felt like I would live forever. Now I'll admit that the weight of the evidence is against that, but this was my first trip. I had just gotten started on life.

We were ready to ride before dawn the next day. We took a packhorse loaded down with flour to make biscuits, and with dry frijole beans, dried fruit, and coffee. Of course, we packed the big load of ammunition and the six-shooter. When I thought we were all set to go Mr. Field said, "Hold on a minute." He went into the house and came out with a Winchester in a scabbard he called a "boot," and I strapped it to my saddle, underneath the leather fender above my stirrup on the right side, with the butt of the rifle forward. He stuffed my saddlebags with ammunition for the Winchester, put some more in the bags on the already overloaded packhorse, and, still not saying anything, walked to his own horse and mounted up. He rode off, headed north. I got on my horse, looped the rope to the packhorse around my saddle horn, and followed him.

The Upper Ranch was in wild-looking country. There had never been a fence anywhere near it. Come to think of it, the only fenced pasture I had ever seen was the horse trap at the Lower Ranch. Of course everyone has heard of the long drift fences out west of here. They went to hell and gone up north and thousands of cattle are said to have drifted south away from the driving cold north wind. Some say that more than one rancher in the Ozona country built his herd from such stock. But that's neither here nor there.

This place was wild and beautiful and like it must have looked a hundred years or more before. You would never think to look at it that the white man had ever found it. The ranch was organized into eight areas. There was a camp with a man stationed in it at each of these eight places, and he was responsible for any cattle on his part of the ranch. Unbranded cattle were to be branded and no more was to be said of it. Juan's camp was in the hills, and this was where we were going.

The Lower Ranch was less than a third the size of this one, but it was in a valley, and the river was wide by the time it got there. No cattle were on it all summer and the grass got high. In the winter most of Mr. Field's livestock were kept in that valley. When spring came there would be a roundup and Mr. Field would divide out what he planned to sell, mark and brand the calves, and then move his breeding stock up to the Upper Ranch, along with the young steers he was fattening up. Grass was scarce in West Texas, especially in the summer, and his herd got spread all over the Upper Ranch. The cowboys said that the fall roundup there, just trying to find as many of the cattle as they could, was misery. Then, driving the cattle over twenty miles through the Clarke ranch was two to three days of dust and hollering and plain old hard work. But it was a good system, rotating the herd between the two ranches.

No matter how they tried they could never get all the cattle that were in the hills and in the cedar brakes and mesquite trees, so there had to be hands working all winter on the Upper Ranch, trying to gather strays and keep them pushed into the different box canyons. Another reason was to make sure folks swinging a wide loop didn't come in and change their brands. When this happened there would be blood on the moon. This was why the owners had to hire hard men for this kind of responsibility. Then, too, there were coyotes and bobcats and wolves, all of which were a menace to the stock, so there was plenty of reason to keep men on the Upper Ranch all through the long, cold winters.

The week we stayed with Juan was a new experience for me. Every morning we would ride until we had covered a certain part of the ranch that was in his territory. Then we would get back to his little one-room cabin before dark and Mr. Field would work with me on gun handling for an hour. After that, while they fixed supper, I would practice another hour. My hand was sore, and I didn't see much progress. It was, to be honest about it, damned discouraging. When Jason Field stood, right arm low, the gun handle out, down on his right side by his hand, he looked like he was frozen, he was that still. Then all of an instant the six-gun would spring up in his hand.

After a few days of this he began to talk about shooting —never to aim, just to point. He would say, "It's just like pointing your finger, it's a natural thing. Never slow down; just work on instinct. Concentrate on your tempo, on your rhythm. Never make a jerky move. Everything has to flow. At first, as you practice, I want you to count under your breath. Build a cadence in your mind." Another time he said, "Don't let yourself get tense; tension is your enemy. Tension breeds fear, it causes your muscles to get tight. Keep your hands firm but relaxed. Don't grip the pistol too tight; all that does is slow you down and hurt your aim. Think how you look. Try for grace and speed. Damn it, Tom, relax those shoulder muscles . . ." He drilled these ideas into my skull. He would show me my mistakes, how I looked—what I was doing wrong. He would have me work on one thing at a time until I had it down pat. Then he would have me work on another. "It's my fault, son, I was taking you too fast." He was the soul of patience and never really got angry.

But no matter how often he showed me I felt awkward.

"You must keep on trying," he said as Juan and he saddled up and left. "Never spend less than two hours a day. Do you hear?" And he left me with a worried look on my face.

CHAPTER 3

The cabin had a dirt floor. I dug a hole and put leaves in it, and then the ground wasn't quite as hard when I slept in my bedroll. But it took a while before I got used to it. Every day seemed to get colder and lonelier. I would practice my draw inside the house, where I had a fire going. The rock chimney drew pretty well, but there were cracks in the boards and when a blue norther hit it was just flat miserable.

Along about this time I got sick of frijoles and dried apricots and beef jerky. I began to hunt, something that has always been a passion with me, and few days passed when I wasn't able to bring down a rabbit or a wild turkey. There weren't many deer, but once in a while I would see one, and then I would spend as much as half a day stalking it. I could forget being lonely, could forget all sense of time, when I was hunting. I wouldn't feel the cold. Nothing on earth existed except me and my quarry. At the kill I would know an ancient, hot joy.

If I do say so, I was a very good shot with the rifle. I still didn't have much confidence in my speed with the handgun, but if a rabbit popped up by the road, the Colt would be in my hand and then the ring of the shot would whang out and the rabbit would be flopping and kicking waist-high in the air, the way they do when you've killed them, but like as not I'd have a private rodeo about that time, unless I was on Bess, because the five horses in the string that Juan had left for me were about half wild. They would get their ears back and head down between their front legs when the shot went off, and then they would fair break in two, as the saying goes. Jesus, but they could buck!

Like I said, I had always had a knack with a rifle, and with practice I got to the point where I just didn't miss. With the pistol it took longer. I found a big old mesquite tree that had a knothole about five feet off the ground, and I would try to hit that knothole. If I rushed I would miss the entire tree. But if I let things flow like Mr. Field had taught me, and watched my rhythm, and concentrated on looking at that knothole and the crusted dark sap that stained the trunk around it, I would hit it nearly every time from ten paces, and without fail from up close.

I had been having nightmares ever since the trouble in Santa Rita. In them I would have my hand on my six-gun's handle and would find myself looking into the barrel of someone else's gun, and I would wake up with a start, with sweat all over. Maybe it was those dreams that made me do it, but I worked my heart out practicing. I'm sure I spent a good bit more than the two hours a day that Mr. Field had advised. I've never been much for work, to tell the truth, but I was in earnest about keeping my young hide unpunctured.

One evening I was chopping firewood out behind the cabin when I heard a wagon in the distance. I stopped and for a moment there were no sounds, and then the noise started again. I could hear slow hoofbeats and the creak of the harness, the jingle of chains, and the rattle the steel-rimmed wheels would make when they hit a patch of rocks. In a minute it pulled up in front of the cabin and a voice called out. I had circled through the shadows of the trees and I walked up, real quiet, behind him.

"Christ almighty! You scared the life out of me!" He hesitated a little, and then he said, "I'm Culley Clarke."

I knew the name. He was the son of Sam Clarke, owner of the Clarke ranch, our neighbor.

"Well," I said, not sure of myself, and realizing it had been some months since I had spoken a solitary word, "get on down and have some coffee." He jumped from the wagon with a laugh and was stretching when I said, "My name's Tom English." It puzzled me when he answered, "I know."

It turned out that he was headed for Villa Plata, a small settlement up the way with a general store that had a bar in it, he said, a livery stable, and maybe eight or ten houses. He was happy to accept my invitation to spend the night, for the cold north wind had a bite to it. And I was happy when he asked me to go along with him to Villa Plata the next day. It was about a twelve-mile ride to the north. When you're seventeen years old it gets weary being alone.

Culley was twenty-four and he was a happy-go-lucky type of cowboy. He was going to pick up some supplies. As a rule, he said, they went to Santa Rita, but for simple things it was a hell of a lot easier to travel to Villa Plata.

We talked the next morning as the springless, rough old wagon bounced and bumped along, and the time flew by for me. I had taken Mr. Field's advice and wasn't wearing the six-gun, but I had it under the seat, wrapped in a gunnysack. If Culley saw the care I took in putting it there he never commented.

Texas weather is freaky at best, and it was warm as it is in late spring as we drove along. The horses were feeling good and Culley had to hold them back. We rode most of the way without talking. The wagon bumped over rocks and mounds of dirt. When we forded the Concho River the horses stopped to drink and breathe. They had their winter coats of thick, long hair and were probably hot. They stood on the gravel bottom of the shallow crossing, with the cold water passing over their legs, and drank deeply, in gulps you could watch travel up their throats. Then they gathered themselves as Culley clucked at them and slapped the reins on their backs, and they lunged and half bucked up the steep angle of the mud bank on the other side. We traveled north and then followed the trail northwest through the Harris ranch. Later, driving toward Villa Plata, we felt refreshed and a little excited. We had on clean clothes, a few dollars were in our pockets, and there was something to do.

In town I had a mug of warm, flat beer while Culley bought the provisions he needed. I was trying to act like I enjoyed the taste when I realized I had a problem. Three cowboys at a table behind me came over to the bar and began staring at me. They were young, and as most people know, young human males can be about as mean and unpredictable as anything on earth.

"It's him, all right. It's the kid who shot Jack Malone." The one talking was small. To my eye he looked like some kind of half-assed idiot, but I was careful not to look at them but for a second or so. Then another, all dressed up, with even a red bandanna around his neck, said, "He ain't carrying no gun." It was the third one I wondered about. He was skinny and ugly and tall. He had one of those vacant faces you see sometimes. I saw that he wore his six-gun low. Taken all together, he made me nervous.

They were drinking the bar's cheap whiskey, though it was not even midafternoon, and they began egging on the tall one with the gun. "Well, Ike, you got your chance with a real gunslinger. You shot that there Meskin last year in what was a fair fight, but he wasn't no match for you."

The two smaller ones kept talking that way to the tall one with the gun, and I could see he was getting upset.

They probably figured I could hear them, and they talked even louder after a while to make damn sure I could. It was about then that I decided I'd better leave.

One of the small ones called after me, "Ike here claims to be the fastest gun who ever walked into Villa Plata." I acted like I didn't hear and I kept walking. Then I heard them following me.

"Turn around and look at me when I talk to you, you hear?" But I went out the door and got in the wagon. The three of them came up and the tall one finally spoke out. He said, "You're a rude son of a bitch, ain't you?"

I could see Culley and five or six people watching. I said, "Mister, I don't know you and you don't know me. As far as politeness goes, I'm the stranger in this town, and I have given no man cause to call me a son of a bitch."

I felt the blood rising up in my face and I understood right then the meaning of the old saying "seeing red." It was like a red haze had settled on the town.

"Gawd damn." The cuss words were drawn out. "Would you look at that yellow-bellied bastard. He's got all flustered, like he's about to cry."

I slapped the reins hard and the horses started off with the wagon. The tall one pulled his pistol out and fired off a shot right in front of the horses, and they reared up and it took me several minutes to quiet them down. Then he said, "Get on out of this town, buster, and don't ever come back —but if you do, you be sure you're packing some iron." He was acting like a big, tough man in front of his friends, running me out of town.

Well, maybe it was that he had been hoorawin' me, or the shot, or maybe because he called me "buster," which is a perfectly good name but he meant it as an insult, and I felt a sense of total rage. There was tension in me that made a tightness in my shoulders and in my hands and arms. I had to clear my head, I had to settle down. I drove down the short main street of Villa Plata and turned the team around. I was behind a one-story frame building, out of sight, and I pulled out my six-gun and put it on the seat next to me, under the gunnysack. Then, slowly and deliberately, giving myself plenty of time to get my concentration, I turned the wagon around and headed back down the street toward the tall fellow who still had his pistol out. He was standing in the center of the road now, in front of the general store. He raised his pistol and pointed it right at me. I had the team of horses turning toward him.

"I said *git*, you son . . ."

He never finished. Looking between the horses' heads it was like I was staring at my tree target with the knothole, and smooth as silk my gun came up, pointed, and exploded; it was like he was yanked backward, head over heels, and he was dead on the instant. I was sure of that.

Thinking back on it I doubt if he saw my hand, what with the horses being between him and me. But to Culley and the other folks it was as if I had drawn on a man pointing a gun at my face.

The two cowboys who had been with the man called Ike were slack-jawed and slobbering as I stepped out of the wagon, the pistol hanging loose in my hand, pointed at the ground. One of them was stuttering and he finally got it out. "Then it's true what they say about Tom English!" I stared at him, wondering, Now what the hell does *that* mean? He and his buddy jumped on their horses and hightailed it out of town before I had a chance to ask him.

I knew I had killed a poor ignorant cowboy who had been out to show off in front of his friends and bluff me into running out of town. In my defense, I hadn't been sure what he might do, but even so I felt downright sick at my stomach.

The folks were whispering and eying each other and me while Culley put the flour and beans and kegs of nails and such like in the wagon bed. Then Culley got up in the driver's seat and I crawled up with him and we rode out of town.

Culley didn't say anything for quite a while. Then he said, "For raw courage I never saw the like of it. There were three of them and one had leveled down on you. How you did it I'll never know." He was still pale as a ghost and was human enough to feel terrible about what had happened.

Later, when it got dark, we stopped and made a fire and warmed up, and ate some salted beef that Culley had. We boiled some coffee and drank it and felt a little better.

"They'll come after you. You can't shoot a man and not expect him to have family or friends who will come to get revenge."

I answered by saying, "I reckon you're right." I am here to confess that I hadn't thought of that part of it, and I was scared, though I tried not to show it.

"Our cowboys told Dad and me about what happened with Malone in Santa Rita, and we knew where you were. Then we got the reports of the hours of shooting practice you were putting in every day. The sound of a pistol shot carries far, and you've been heard—and you've been watched. Well"—he broke off with a laugh—"there ain't no ordinary cowpoke going to interfere with a gunslinger, so the folks watching you didn't make a courtesy call."

"Lord, Lord, Lord," Culley kept breathing out loud when we got back in the wagon. And he was still talking like that when we got to Juan's old cabin. Culley told me to come on over to the Clarke headquarters if trouble came, for they had twelve cowhands there. Then he said, "Come on over even if no trouble comes. It has to be lonely for you here."

I appreciated that and told him I would. That night I couldn't sleep, so after a time I got my bedroll, my pistol, and the Winchester and climbed up the hill to a cave I'd found, in among some boulders. In the summer it probably would be cool and as a result alive with rattlesnakes, but it was still early March, and rattlers hibernate until the days get warm.

I built a small fire and rolled up in my sleeping bag. It was cold but suddenly I was bone-tired. I wouldn't be eighteen years old for three months and I had already killed two men who really didn't have a chance and I knew it. I felt a deeper fear than any I'd ever known, and I tried to pray and tell the Lord I was sorry, but I couldn't find the words. It's hard to pray with a Colt .45 in your hand, yet I didn't dare put it away. In the end I gave it up and at last I went to sleep.

CHAPTER 4

No one came. I was on the lookout for six weeks, but not a soul showed up to try to revenge the death I had caused. After all of this time I was aware that I was about to get spooked, so I rode over to the Clarke ranch one Sunday and they received me well. Some of the cowboys looked wary, for I was wearing the six-gun full time now, and the Winchester was in its boot on my saddle. But Culley was delighted to see me. He introduced me to his father and mother, and to Agnes and Sally Clarke, his two younger sisters. The youngest of the family, Sally, brought us a plate of cookies and some coffee.

I kept watching her. She appeared to be my age, and was a skinny little thing, but she had a surprisingly full chest, although I shouldn't have looked there, and I certainly am no gentleman for commenting about it. I was tongue-tied whenever either of the girls came into the room, and Culley teased me some about that in a good-natured way. Even Mr. Sam Clarke had to smile. "Tom," he said, "you may not know it but there are folks who tell tales about you, about how fearless you are and all. Surely you're not bothered by one or two young girls."

Well, Culley whooped at that, and I spilled some coffee. But it wasn't an unpleasant feeling. It was like they had accepted me. After being all by myself for so long I was hungry to be with people, and I was aware that I was sitting there grinning like a chessie cat.

Later we walked out to the corral and looked at a new stud Mr. Clarke had bought. He was over seventeen hands high, and had a thick, powerful neck and chest. He was by all odds the biggest horse I had ever seen outside of work-horses. He was a bay color and was as gentle as a pony. Mr. Clarke had named him Dan.

The day was dark with clouds in the west and every now and then we would see chain lightning, and then we'd hear the low rolling boom of the thunder. The wind got up and there was a marvelous fresh smell.

There are few happier times in West Texas than when it rains. It may be so common many places that folks get tired of it, but out here it is so rare that when it comes it is like the land is being renewed. The people too. Well, of course, with the storm, nothing would do but that I must spend the night.

I waked up three or four times, there in the guest room, wondering where I was. It seemed unnatural, sleeping in the softness of a real bed after so long. I would lie there, still, and listen to the sound of the rain slashing against the windowpanes and hammering softly on the roof, hour after hour.

The next morning Sally, the young one I may have mentioned, fixed my breakfast. Flapjacks and fried eggs and a glass of milk and hot coffee.

"You're mighty thin," she said, and for an instant she touched my arm. I looked up, surprised, and she blushed and went back to the stove.

We walked out and saw cochineal bugs, little dots that seemed like bright red velvet, that only came out after a rain.

Sally Clarke rode part of the way with me when I left, and I asked if I could come back to see her. She said yes, she guessed so. Just a simple sentence. People say things like that all the time, so I don't know why I was so dad-blamed pleased with myself.

I rode along daydreaming and lollygagging, and then, just as I got to the camp, I was brought up short. It took a minute before I could accept what I saw. Juan's cabin was burned halfway down. I saw it before I got there, and I tied my horse and ran with my rifle from bush to bush and rock to rock, like I did when I was trying to stalk a deer, but no one was around.

I went back for my horse and we edged through the mesquite and made a wide circle. When I was satisfied that nobody was there, and no one was hiding up in the rocks of the hill where the cave was, I found that the extra horses had been scattered as well as the strays that I had gathered during the long winter.

Whoever it was must have come the day before, for it looked like the rain had put out the fire. But the place was beyond fixing. Any tracks that might have been left behind had been washed out.

I went to the cave to think about my problems. Lucky for me, I had all my provisions there, as well as my bedroll, so the loss of the cabin was not too bad. I had moved out of it six weeks before anyway.

The next few days I was able to round up the horses and nearly all the stray cattle that had been scattered, so I was busy from dawn till dark—from "can see" to "can't see," as the cowboys sometimes said.

Then I went to Villa Plata. I had waited for people to come to me long enough. If there was to be trouble we might as well get on with it. I was going to be available for the man who had come out and burned Juan's shack. The more I thought about it the madder I got.

The town was quiet late that afternoon when I arrived. I put my mare in the livery stable and gave her some oats as well as hay and water. I left the saddle and bridle on, but I loosened the girth so she could breathe easy.

Then I took the Winchester in my left hand and I walked over to the general store. The bartender recognized me right off. It was then that I got called "mister" for the first time in my life. "What'll you have, Mr. English?" Well, I had a beer. Then I asked him if anyone had been looking for me, and he said that five men had come in the week before, and my whereabouts was all they had in mind. This set me back on my heels, all right. I had expected to have it out with one man.

The bartender, whose name was Coot Snyder, was a talkative old cuss with a long mustache and side-whiskers. He had a gravelly-sounding voice and it struck me that he was well suited to his work. He seemed to dearly love to pour whiskey and was disappointed that, like most folks, I took beer instead. He even pulled out a bottle of his private stock from underneath the bar, but I explained that I had only tasted whiskey once before, and that the memory of it was such that I didn't plan to try it again soon. Of course, I was thinking of Malone's bar, but there was no way for him to understand that, so he looked puzzled and a little hurt. Then he remembered the five men and he began to talk about them.

"Four of them were kin of Ike Phillips, the man you shot here." He hesitated.

"Who was the fifth man?"

He poured himself a drink before he answered. Then he just said the name, "Joe Slade."

It was as though someone had thrown a glass of water in my face. Joe Slade was, without much doubt, the meanest man in West Texas.

Coot Snyder began to tell stories about him. There was one in particular that he dwelt on. A similar tale had been told about John Wesley Hardin, but he doubted the truth of it. However, he said that he had firsthand knowledge in the case of Joe Slade, and he was sure of his facts. Then he related the story that I had already heard, about the time that Slade had shot a Mexican boy dead, and later explained it was just to see him kick. Then Coot told how Slade would badger a scared cowboy into a fight and then gun him down. He had done this so often that people were sick with fear when they heard his name.

"Why would he look for me?"

"Hell, everyone has been talking about you. About how you practice for hours every day. This is a mighty big country, but there ain't much to do out here but drink and talk when you ain't workin'." He broke off for a minute, and then he went on. "I reckon he wants to take you while he still can. He's not gettin' any younger and with time a man can get a little slower."

Coot Snyder looked me in the eyes and said, with his funny rough voice, "You're not ready for him, boy. Joe Slade is faster than greased lightning. He's faster than a rattlesnake in midstrike."

Just at that moment we heard the sound of horses pulling up and I saw some men tying them to the hitching rail. I looked at Coot's face and was surprised at how pale it was all of a sudden. Then he whispered, "Speak of the devil: it's Ike Phillips's kin, and Joe Slade is with them."

CHAPTER 5

There wasn't time to run, though I'm here to tell you I ain't too proud to light a shuck when it looks necessary. Without no question at all it looked necessary.

The five men came into the bar and ordered whiskey. Two were the small young fellows who had been with the man I had shot. The other two were older and shaggy-looking, like they hadn't shaved in quite a while. The fifth had to be Joe Slade. He was medium-sized and trim. He was dressed like the rest except his six-gun was lower on his leg than any I had ever seen. He didn't have to slant his gun belt that far down because he had a special long loop on his holster. He held his drink with his left hand and his right was even with the butt of his gun.

It was peculiar but, instead of being scared, I found myself wondering if a man could shave a piece of a second off his draw time with a rig like that. Then the two young punks saw me. They jerked back like wasps had stung them, and then they began whispering and pointing. The five men spread apart and fanned out across the room.

I don't know what possessed me, for it seemed that I was watching what happened. The fear was gone and that old monster, rage, crawled up. I have never been able to stand being crowded. I heard my voice, cold as iron, say, "Joe Slade, I reckon you've lost your nerve, hiding behind these cowpokes." (I may have been bold but I wasn't stupid enough to say what I thought about his choice of companions.) I kept on: "I've come in to see you personal. I'm looking for a man who would sneak around and burn a cabin and steal horses."

His mouth was straight across and then he curled it into something like a smile, except his black eyes were hard. He said, "You killed Jack Malone and Ike Phillips. They were good friends."

"I didn't know you had friends."

Slade's eyes began to glitter. He said, "I'm going to take this son of a bitch. Don't none of you do a damn thing." Then, staring at me, the half smile left his face and his eyes looked crazy. It was like he was trying to scare me, the way some snakes do with their victims, so they'll be helpless. From what Coot had said this had worked for him before. Slade said, "Come on out in the street, Tom Tricks."

The old red haze closed in as he kept talking. "Tricky Tom, who bushwacked Jack Malone, who shot Ike Phillips from behind some horses. Come on outside in the sun. This time there ain't no fancy Dan stunts you can pull."

Joe Slade looked taller than he had before. He kept his eye fixed on me and he backed out the door and into the street. My mouth was bone-dry and there was this terrible excitement in the pit of my stomach. I could feel my pulse pounding in my ears.

I walked out the door and saw he was in the west, with the sun square behind him. He was one for calculation, there was no doubt about that. I crossed the street and stood facing him, close to the livery stable. From that angle the sun wasn't too bad, and I started toward him. This time I had no surprises. I wasn't holding my gun under a gunnysack or drawing on a man choked up with laughter. I was still astonished by my total lack of fear. All I felt was a terrible coldness.

There wasn't a question of someone saying, "Draw," or

anything like that. With your life on the line you don't worry about politeness. Slade drew his gun without any warning. I say he drew it but there wasn't any start to the draw. The first thing I saw was his gun coming up in his hand and then I heard a roar.

It was an instant before I realized it had been my gun. The bullet hit him in the left side and spun him half around. My gun went off twice more as he staggered. The last shot kicked him over backward. Just then something slammed into me from behind and threw me facedown. I had been shot in the back. I rolled over and came up on one knee. The two boys had their six-guns out and bullets were flying every whichaway. A shot hit me in the leg and another in the left arm. I pulled back up and shot quick. First one and then the other. They went down side by side, like they had been axed.

The older two stood there, gray-faced, empty-handed. Then Coot Snyder came out with my rifle in his hands. I heard him say "No more." I felt myself slide down into the dusty street. The pain in my back stretched up into my head. I tried to call out to Coot, then everything turned dark.

Pain did it. I came back to being half conscious. Coot was wrapping my three wounds up tight to try to stop the bleeding. I heard a man say, "I'll take him to the Clarke ranch. They're friends of his. Maybe they can get the doctor from Santa Rita."

Another said, "He ain't goin' to make it."

I heard some other voices. One was excited, yelling out, "Tom English just shot two of Ike Phillips's cousins, and he got Joe Slade too. He killed the meanest man in West Texas." Another person said, "Well, if he lives, I reckon he can have the title hisself. Hell of an honor, ain't it?" Off in the distance I heard a voice saying, "Tom English killed three men before you could blink your eyes."

Things after that were mixed up. I was in a wagon, and the pain was more than I could stand. Then I don't remember anything much, just the sounds of people talking. Once I heard myself moan and I looked up at a man in a dark coat with whiskers. He said, "It's all right now, son. I got the bullet from your back. The others passed clean through."

Then I looked at some curtains ruffle in the warm spring breeze and I saw the sun's top rim at break of day. I was so weak I couldn't do more than open my eyes. Then a lady's voice, it turned out to be Mrs. Clarke, said, "He's conscious."

She put her cool hands on my face and smoothed my hair. It had been a mighty long time since I had felt anything like that.

Later she and Agnes and Sally plumped up my pillows and brought in some flowers. They put some roses in a vase, and then they brought me hot soup to eat.

I had been there almost a week and they had tended to me. This is very embarrassing for me to tell. There I was, under the cover, without a stitch on. I have absolutely never been so mortified in all my born life.

Sally came each day and read to me. Agnes was real kind to me except she teased me a good bit about how Sally was making eyes at me. I was able to dress and sit up now, and the pain wasn't as bad. One day Sally trimmed my hair and pressed up against me. It seemed to me like she did that on purpose. I guess it was because I was weak but I got tears in my eyes. She saw them and her eyes filled up too. She sat beside me on the bed and very gently put her arms around me, saying, "There, there," like a mother does to a little boy who has been hurt.

The day after that we had a surprise. Jason Field came to see me. He and the cowboys from the Lower Ranch were moving the herd through to the Upper Ranch.

He sat in a straight chair in the room and rolled a cigarette. "I got the news two days ago, Tom. I would have come over right off if I had known. This is terrible." I didn't know what to answer, but he kept on talking. "I've heard some mighty bad things, Tom."

"I'm afraid they're true, Mr. Field."

"Well, there is no way for you to stay in this part of the country now. Every gunsel in Texas will want to take you when you're not expecting it. I know what I'm talking about. You've been written up in the newspapers. Ben Jordan, the U.S. marshal, has talked to me, and he knows you didn't start these fights. But he told me that when he gets to this part of his circuit he is going to have to ask you to ride on."

We were both quiet. Then he spoke again, and his voice was husky. "I can see myself in you and I know how you feel. I was on the run when I came here thirty years ago."

Still I didn't say anything. I just couldn't find the words.

Mr. Field looked at me and said, "It just isn't fair. By God, I'm going to talk to Ben Jordan when I find him. Maybe we can work something out."

He rose and smiled. "Sam tells me his daughter Sally thinks you can do no wrong. Why not try to live up to her image of you?" He kept standing there. After a time he said, "One of these days I hope you will settle down and have a family. Living by yourself goes against the grain. It's hard being alone when you're old." Then he left. But what he said affected me.

I thought about it when Sally brought me supper and then later as she rubbed my head. She said, "When you were brought in you kept asking about Bess." There was an awkward long pause. "Is that your girlfriend?"

I grinned up at her and said, "No, ma'am, Bess is my horse." She laughed too and leaned down real quick and, to my considerable surprise, kissed me right on the mouth.

CHAPTER 6

I sat on the bank of the Concho and watched Culley light a stick of dynamite with a short fuse. He looked at it for half a second to make sure it was lit, and then he flung it out into the middle of the river. A moment later it went off underwater, and there was an eruption of mud, water, rocks, and fish. I couldn't believe my eyes. There were dead fish floating all over the water when it finally calmed down. Howling with glee Culley ran down the bank and jumped in the water, clothes and all. He threw out sun perch, bass, catfish, and one long old gar with fearsome teeth. He got over twenty of the best on a stringer and left the rest on the bank for the buzzards.

"We're going to have ourselves a fish fry tonight," Culley hollered as we went to get our horses.

I was stiff and sore but was getting better fast. It was a Sunday and Culley had been bound and determined to show me how to blast for fish. My idea of fishing was a good bit more serene than Culley's, but his was certainly more effective, although there sure was no sport to it. When we got back to the house Culley went in to clean the fish and I went to the guest room that they called "Tom's room." It was time to start practicing once more. The bad dreams had begun again. In my nightmares I would draw as slow as molasses, and there I would be, hand on my gun butt, looking down a barrel. The same old dream.

Sally was out by the corral when I got there and I saw

her eyes go down toward my six-gun. I explained about the need to practice, but she couldn't understand. She frowned and complained, but when I got my horse she said, "Wait for me."

It was a pleasure to see her go into that corral. She was in man's pants and had a rope, and she built a loop just like a man does, mostly with a wrist flip, and she caught a horse without wasting a single motion. I came over to help her saddle up, but she had it on before I could give her a hand.

Then we were riding together and I listened to her chatter about all kinds of foolishness. When we got to the hills, well off from the house, we tied our horses to a hackberry tree. My leg and arm were all right but the wound in my back had affected my left shoulder and arm. They were stiff and still hurt. I felt in luck that the right arm was not affected.

I stopped before a tree and set my mind, wondering just how rusty I had gotten in a month. Then the tree was like a man throwing down on me, and I drew.

The six shots roared out on top of each other and, looking at the tree, I was satisfied to see that they were grouped together. They had torn out a piece of the tree about six inches across. There was smoke coming out of the Colt's muzzle as I reloaded. Was the draw slow? It always seemed too slow.

It doesn't take long to form a habit. Just a few weeks. My practicing may have been driven by fear but there was more to it than that. As I got the hang of it the drudgery had stopped. It was remarkable to me to be able to see the results of my efforts. I could feel the improvement. It is a peculiar thing, setting a task for your body that is difficult. When you get your muscles and your reflexes trained there is an animal satisfaction, as much physical as mental. I seem to be going on and on about this, but it was a very big part of my life. Pride was a part of it, too. I knew I was better than most. It was heady to me to think that there was one thing that I could do better than practically anyone on earth. Even with this, every time I practiced I had the feeling that I could improve. This, the pride, and the bad dreams drove me. I would have been ashamed to tell Sally why I felt funny if I went a day without this strange kind of work.

I had never heard of anyone else practicing on a daily basis. No one talked of the well-known gunfighters doing this. It struck me that they probably made it on natural ability and quick reflexes, together with the fact that they were cooler, they could concentrate better, and the men up against them were full of nerves or whiskey or both. Well, I felt that my concentration was as good as most, and I knew I had good reflexes and natural coordination. It seemed that if I *worked* at gun handling I would have to be more than the equal of the folks who depended on nothing but their basic quickness and meanness. That was my excuse, that and the fear.

I had reloaded and was facing the target tree when I heard a noise. I looked around and saw that Sally was about to cry. She looked terrible. She wasn't being flirtatious.

I held her and felt grown-up and protective. Actually, I'm only about five foot ten but she is not more than five foot one or two, so she held on tight with her head down on my chest. I holstered my gun and then, I couldn't help it, I just hugged her right back.

She asked, "Aren't you going to kiss me?" And I said, "Well, of course I am." I took off her hat and my hat and threw them on the ground. Her eyes were closed and her face was held up to me and all of a sudden I felt an emotion that is beyond me to describe. I did it. I hauled off and kissed her good and proper. She held on to me and that was the end of that day's target practice. We even held hands riding back to the ranch house, until we got where people might see us.

While we were unsaddling the horses she stared at me like she was going to eat me up with her eyes. It was very confusing, but I felt about as happy as I ever have in my life.

When we got to the main house Jason Field was there, and he had brought the U.S. marshal, Ben Jordan, with him. Culley came up about that time with his dad, and the five of us went into the parlor. The womenfolk left us.

The marshal sat down, put his hat on the floor beside him, and looked at me after we got settled in our chairs. Culley fixed a glass of whiskey for everyone but me, for he knew I hadn't acquired the taste. As a matter of fact, I couldn't abide it. He brought me a glass of water and grinned at me.

The marshal said, "There are no charges against you, young man. Everything that has happened in the last year has been damned unfortunate, but fair and square. The hell of it is that you are going down a road that will be your end. I don't care how good you are now, or how much better you may get to be. Too many are going to be out to get you. No"—he shook his head—"practicing won't keep you alive. I know what I'm talking about. I've lived by the gun all of my life."

It felt like there was a lump of ice in my chest. I hope I didn't show it, but his words sunk home.

It was then that old man Sam Clarke spoke up. He said, "I have a suggestion to make. We own a small ranch about two hundred miles from here. It's at the end of the earth, over by the Mexican border, between Sanderson and Langtry. It never has made me any money for the place is too handy for the rustlers from across the border. At the same time, it has possibilities. Right now I only have three men working out there. If we could get things under control the ranch might amount to something, though it is mighty rough country."

I jumped at the chance. At least no one would know me. It would be a fresh start. Mr. Clarke said, "Don't be thanking me, boy, the Circle X is a damned dangerous place to be. But it's possible that you would be better off than here."

So, with me just sitting there, I got talked about like I was invisible, and they decided it was for the best.

Mr. Field said, "Tom, you've become something of a big name in the last year. Around here it's just a matter of time before some crazy kid will gun you down from the dark, or from behind." He smiled, "I don't reckon you'll get called out soon again. They won't be anxious to face you head on. It strikes me that this job on the border would be just the thing for you."

Ben Jordan got up. He was a big man but old. It took him a while to straighten his back. He said, "Your picture has been in the papers. It is a drawing that some yahoo made, but it is a fair likeness. You need to look different. Can you grow a mustache?"

They all laughed and I could feel my face getting hot, and they laughed even more. I never have been able to keep from showing my feelings. I said, "Well, I never tried, but I can sure give it a go." They teased me some more about that, and Marshal Jordan said, "You just do that."

About that time we smelled the fish frying, and Culley told the story of the great dynamite explosion, waving his arms around. That Culley could sure talk. It sounded even better as he told it than it had been at the time. Everyone in the room was in a real good humor except for me. I already felt alone. I missed Sally like crazy and she was just in the next room.

Sam Clarke could see I was down in the mouth and I reckon he set out to cheer me up. "Tom, I've been thinking of that ranch on the border. There's not much we can do to improve the longhorns. They can live on land that horned toads would starve on. We're beginning to experiment here with the Hereford breed from England, and with time I think we will all go in that direction. They turn grass into fine beef. They are simply more efficient than any other breed I've seen. We have good buffalo grass here. But only longhorns can survive on the Circle X."

I had seen the stocky red, white-faced cattle he was talking about, but the very idea of a cow being efficient was a thought that had never crossed my mind. Mr. Clarke went on, "I think we might do worse than work on improving our horseflesh. That's why I bought Dan in Kansas City. I want you to take him out to the Circle X and put him with the mares we've got there. Then, in about six months, I want you to bring him back."

Well, I was flattered at the trust he was showing me. I knew how much store he put by Dan. All of a sudden I felt mighty good. A little self-respect can make a heap of difference in how the world looks.

CHAPTER 7

I packed as carefully as I could. I was riding Bess and leading Dan and a gray packhorse, name of Paco. I took a good supply of provisions and plenty of ammunition for my six-gun and the Winchester. Culley put a few sticks of dynamite in for me to try out in the Rio Grande. He said, "As big and long as that river is, God only knows the size of the catfish."

It was before dawn and still dark when I left, though the sky in the east was a funny pale lavender. I was headed west, where the sky was still as black as the ace of spades. When I got to the rise I stopped for one last look. It was light enough by then to make out the main house and the bunkhouse and barn, and all the pens and corrals. Then I saw a pony coming toward me from the ranch, lickety-split. In a minute I saw it was Sally riding bareback like an Indian. She pulled up in a cloud of dust and spooked Dan a second. He half reared up. I was talking to him when she walked up and said, "Get down off of that horse, cowboy." When I did she grabbed me around the neck and kissed me. Then she grinned and jumped on her pony and said, "I don't want you to let a day go by without thinking of me." At that she galloped back toward the house. As she rode she turned and waved.

Five days later I figured I should be getting close, but to tell the truth, I didn't know where I was. Then I came to the Pecos River and I followed it as it looped south to the

Rio Grande. I camped that night in a pocket of trees just off the water. Cliffs were behind me and were on the other side too, for the river had cut a deep canyon at this particular place. I had found a steep, twisting trail that made a sharp descent—at times for a foot or two it was almost vertical—to the river. I followed it, leaning back on Bess while she picked her way down. Then I sat and looked for a long time. It was the quietest place I had ever been. The cliffs seemed to cut off all sound and there was nothing to hear but an occasional river noise. Once or twice an owl hooted.

The next morning I fished for a time with no luck. It was funny to sit there and look across the river and realize that over there, right before me, was Old Mexico. Along about midday I headed out, and it was a scrambling ride over the loose rocks on the trail, until we got to the top. I figured if I followed the Rio Grande as it meandered west and northwest I would find Langtry before too long, and they could tell me the best way to get to the Circle X.

Later I came across a Mexican cowboy wearing a big sombrero and spurs with oversized rowels. They were as big around as silver dollars and were pointed, not dull like spurs should be.

He was a hard-looking man, riding a pinto that looked plumb wore out. On top of that there were tracks of dried blood where he had been spurred. I had been traveling slow and easy and my horses were fat and rested. He kept looking at Dan and saying things in his language that I couldn't understand. When I said, "Langtry," he brightened up and waved to show that I was to follow him.

It was late in the day when we got to the town, if you could call it that. There wasn't a hell of a lot to see. There was an old store and down a ways from it was a mesquite tree with a man sitting on the ground under it. Then I saw he was chained to the tree. I'd heard about the open-air Langtry jail and there it was.

When we rode up in front of the store the dust blew on the people on the front porch, and they glared at me. There was one old man with a full beard that was yellow and white and streaked with tobacco juice. He said he was Judge Roy Bean. I'd heard a few tales about him, but I wasn't prepared for his appearance. If ever I saw a man who needed a bath he was the one. He was absolutely the dirtiest, the filthiest-looking old son of a bitch I ever seen. The six Mexicans on the porch in front of the store were dirty too, and all of them looked mean as homemade sin. You never saw so many cartridge belts. One man had two crossed over his chest and another around his waist.

I stepped off Bess and nodded as polite as I knew how, and went up on the porch to see if the judge could tell me where the Circle X was. I even took my hat off. He sat there and stared at me and acted like he hadn't heard me.

"I was sayin' that I work for Mr. Sam Clarke. I'm on the way to his ranch, the Circle X west of here, and I'd be much obliged if you could help me with some directions."

"You'll have to wait a little."

"What for?"

"You got to wait till we hang that man yonder chained to the tree."

I explained to him that I wasn't one for that kind of sight, and I started to go down the steps. The judge's men were looking at Dan. They gathered around him and Dan's neck bowed up and he backed away from them. He made quite a picture. I couldn't help but be proud. Then the judge's voice cracked out like a whip, "Where'd you steal that horse?"

I felt my damned old face swell up with blood, and my mouth began to tremble. I would give anything if I could keep that from happening. It seems like I get mad in a split second, and it always shows.

"I didn't steal no horse. This here is the property of Mr. Sam Clarke and, like I said, I'm taking him to the Circle X ranch."

"No," he said and his voice was harsh and real deliberate, "you ain't. I figure you for a horse thief just like the one we got chained to that mesquite tree." Then he banged a whiskey bottle down on top of a barrel that was next to the cane-bottom chair he was sitting in. "Guilty!" I looked up, real surprised, and he said it again, and in the cruelest way you ever heard, "Guilty. We're going to hang you too."

I had braided the tie-downs on my holster but it only took a few seconds to loosen them, and as he was talking I tied the holster down to my right leg. I straightened up and said, "Judge, my name is Tom English. Which one of your men wants to make the first move?"

I had never used my name, my reputation, before and it was astonishing how well it worked. His gunhands may not have understood much of what I was saying, but they could spot a gunfighter, and they knew the name of Tom English.

The judge hesitated just a fraction of a second and said, "I don't believe you," and he nodded toward a man off to one side. It must have been a signal, for that fellow started toward his gun but then stopped. My six-gun was on his face before his hand had a hold of the butt of his gun, and he froze there and real slowly raised his hands. The others sucked in and said things like *"Madre de Dios!"*

I put my pistol back in the holster and pointed a finger with my left hand at each man in turn. "You?" I'd wait with my right hand low, and when he kept standing there like a post, I would point to the next and then the next, "You?" When I'd gone clear down the line and had pointed at the last man the judge began to laugh. "You're a good one, you are." He stopped laughing and said, "I fancy that big bay stud. What'll you take for him?"

"He ain't mine to sell, Judge." I got on Bess and said, "I'll tell you what I *will* do. If you'll turn that fellow loose you are fixing to hang I'll promise to give you one of his colts. I expect his colts will be finer than anything in this part of the country." I could see him think about it, so I kept on. "This bay stallion has a bloodline that goes clear back to England." That seemed to do the trick, for he rattled off some Spanish and two of his men unchained the bewildered, scared man under the tree. I watched while he headed off toward the Rio Grande and Mexico. He wasn't questioning what had happened. I waited until he had a good start. It was getting dark and he would be hard to find. Then I said, "You'll get the first colt, Judge," and rode off before they got their nerve up.

I still didn't know exactly where the Circle X was but I figured I'd prefer to wander west along the Rio Grande than to stay in Langtry.

CHAPTER 8

The cowboys at the Circle X were real glad to see me. I didn't take that as too much of a compliment, because they were so lonesome and hungry for news that it was downright pathetic. I could tell they had heard my name and were impressed by it, which was embarrassing in one way and a little heady in another. None of them let on that he knew much about me, but they looked me over with some care.

The next morning we put Dan out with the mares and cut out of the herd of wild horses four of the best-looking ones to go in my string.

From then on it was rodeo time whenever I saddled up, except for the days I rode Bess. I was throwed more than once, I'll have to admit. The first time my horse bucked right through an outside fire where most of the cooking was done. A coffeepot went one way, a skillet another, and hot coals scattered all around. Then I flew off into a patch of prickly pear. Lord, how those cowboys laughed. It took a week before I got all the cactus spines out.

Because I was younger and had raw horses to ride they all got a hell of a kick out of me. The cowboys would offer to swap me their horses, which were well broke by now. But I said, "No, you've done what I'm going through now, so I'll just have to stick with it." Of course, in a month it all worked out. I will say that I learned more about bronc riding in that month than I had ever learned before. It has to be done with balance and anticipation of what the horse is going to try next. You can't outmuscle a horse. I had thought of myself as a pretty good rider, but I got that piece of foolishness jolted loose right quick. Anyway, like I was saying, after a month the horses found they couldn't buck me off, so they stopped trying. It was something of a disappointment to the three men and, though it may sound strange, to me too. It had sort of livened up the day.

One thing I did late each afternoon was to ride off to a canyon not too far from our camp and practice a lot with my timing with the six-gun. I would draw and shoot from all sorts of positions. I even practiced left-handed but it was awkward. If I braced my left hand with the pistol over my right forearm I was fairly accurate, but it wasn't the same as my "pointing" system with the right hand.

I practiced with the Winchester some, but not often. On the other hand I did go deer hunting fairly often. They had black-tailed deer in this country that were half again as big as the white-tailed deer I had been used to hunting at the Upper Ranch.

The cowboys, Lon, Slocum, and Joe Bob, could hear the racket I made with the Colt but, though I could see they were curious, they never asked me about it, and I couldn't very well tell them that if I missed a day the bad dreams would start. I never had thought of myself before as one who just had to do something. I had been mighty free and easy before, but for some time now I had what you might call an obsession. That is to say, something was driving me. I don't know why I keep trying to explain this. Maybe so I'll understand it myself. I guess I should admit to being scared, though this is something I would never say out loud.

Several times, out hunting, I would see Mexican cowpunchers who may or may not have been rustlers. I'd let them see I was watching them from the distance and they would ride on.

The unspoken agreement was that the three cowboys did most of the work looking after the longhorns and the horses, and I patrolled to keep an eye out for rustlers. It made sense to them for this had been the big problem on the Circle X. Sometimes I would wake and saddle up before daylight. I would ride out to the herd and stay in the scrub trees, or on the rocky hills, looking for trouble. But we were lucky for none came our way.

The cowboys commented that the word must be out that I was there, for they had been losing stock across the border right up until I arrived, and then it stopped.

I had been at the Circle X almost four months when it happened. We waked up to find ourselves short around fifty longhorns and six mares. But the worst of it was that they had taken Dan, Mr. Clarke's prize studhorse. I could never face him if I lost that horse, but I had to see him if I was to be with Sally again. I know that doesn't sound too logical, but I was still in my teens and at that age you don't always have good sense. At any rate I had sure been thinking of Sally every day and the thought of not seeing her again was more than I could bear. There was no choice in my mind about what had to be done.

There was a good deal of choice as far as the three cowboys were concerned. They kept saying, "Risk my hide in Mexico? For another man's horse?" They could see me getting real mad and after a while Joe Bob, who was a little older than the others, said, "Well, hell, if Tom is bound to go, I'll ride along to keep him company." After that the other two said they might as well tag along. Then they all got to laughing, maybe to get their nerve up.

Lon, who had been the most reluctant, said, "If this turns into a gunfight I'm going to hightail it for Texas." I said, "You all are along to herd the cattle. There has to be a way to get hold of them. Maybe we can drive them off as easy as they did. The Mexicans may not guard them too well once they feel they've got away safe." I could see he wasn't convinced and I reckon I was a little vague as to just how we were going to get a hold of the cattle and Dan too.

The four of us crossed the Rio Grande into Mexico just at high noon. From the tracks it appeared that there were at least ten men we were up against, and they didn't have that much of a lead. Driving the stock would naturally slow them down a good bit.

Outnumbered the way we were we hung back and took our time. It would be better for them to think they had gotten away with it. After all, no one from the Circle X had ever chased after them before, so maybe they wouldn't be expecting it this time.

On the other hand, likely as not they would leave lookouts behind. The boys were asking me what we should do. They took it for granted that I would know, and I had to act like I did. Working on the hunch that they wouldn't leave lookouts for too long, we stopped by a little creek that ran northeast to the Rio Grande and unsaddled. We camped there that afternoon and night. It was downright eerie for some reason—maybe because we kept wondering if we were being watched, or maybe it was because we were in a foreign country.

The trail was easy enough to follow when we rode out the next morning, although the ground was rocky. I'll never know if scouts had been left behind, but if there had been any they had gone by the time we came along.

In the late afternoon we went through a pass between some craggy mountains and after a little we topped a rise and saw a small valley below us. Our cattle were at one end of it, with three men on horseback looking after them. At the other end of the valley there was a large old adobe house with other men moving around beside it. There was a fire and it appeared women were there, cooking. As we watched we could make out more women and several children. The rustlers' horses and those they had stolen were in a corral behind the house. There were two old tents pitched behind the house, where apparently some of the people stayed. We got off our horses down behind the ridge, out of sight of the Mexicans, and the men looked at me. Joe Bob asked, "Now what?"

I shoved my hat back and hunkered down on my boots, sort of sitting on my heels the way cowboys do. They did the same thing. "Well," I said finally, "you fellows stay here. I'll work my way around these hills and see if I can't get behind the three with the cattle. Then I'll try to get the longhorns spooked. If they stampede you can pick them up and head them toward Texas."

We all knew that turning a stampede wasn't that simple, but in the daytime with only fifty cattle it could be brought off.

"What about the three men? We goin' to take them back to Texas with us?" Slocum had a wry way about him.

"No, of course not. If I'm down behind those rocks I should be able to hit their horses with my rifle. I hate to do it, but I can't think of no other way. That ought to get the cattle going."

"Then what?"

"While you all get the cattle moving out, I'll stay hidden until the others from the house come after you. They'll hear the shots and you can count on company pretty quick. I'll ride for their corral, get Dan and switch saddles, then I'll start shooting and raising hell to drive off the rest of the horses. Unless I miss my guess the rustlers will figure we've attacked their camp and they will come back to protect their womenfolk and their kids."

It was amazing how they took all this in. I was younger than they were by a good bit, but they seemed to think this was something I knew about and, above all, they were glad to have someone tell them exactly what to do.

"What if they don't turn back?"

"Then leave the cattle and light a shuck for Texas. Their horses will be winded and you can get away easy."

Lon looked real worried. He asked, "What about you, Tom?"

"If they turn back or if they don't, once I'm on Dan they'll never catch me. In a high lope he can leave behind any horse they have ever had at a dead run. Besides, their horses will damn sure be winded if they barrel back down the valley right after running up it."

"You may have it figured, Tom, but the whole thing looks risky as all get-out to me."

I have wished a hundred times I had listened to him. I had no idea what a terrible mess I was getting into.

We were up against hard men, men who lived with guns and knives. There would be no bluffing them. We all had heard of the cruel things they had done and we knew there would be no mercy if we got caught. Though no one said it, each man jack of us vowed silently not to be taken alive. Lon kept muttering, "This ain't what I bargained for." Joe Bob asked him, "Do you want to trade jobs with Tom?" And Lon answered, "Hell, no!"

I rode in a long, meandering direction, behind hills that were lining the valley, staying out of sight so I couldn't be seen. It took me over an hour but I finally got behind the three men with the cattle. I tied my horse and crept up the hill, going from one bush to the next until I got to the crest. They were right below me, down a gentle grade that wasn't near as steep as the one I had just climbed. One was not a hundred yards away but the others were a good bit off. I figured if I shot the horse of the one closest to me the others might run. My plan was coming apart.

It was then that I acted on a damn fool hunch. I stood up where they could see me and shot in the air to scare the cattle. I thought all three would head toward me and I would have time to get down in the rocks and knock their horses down with my Winchester.

At the instant of my shot they did bolt for me. That's the last thing that worked like I thought it would. They came in fast from three directions, one of them looping wide out of my range. Just then a ricochet whined off a rock next to me and another shot splattered rock chips all over me. There was no time to think. I whipped off a shot with the Winchester at the closest man and missed. His horse seemed to be flying. He was almost on top of me and I dropped the rifle and threw down on him with the Colt. During this time he and his pardner were shooting at me as fast as they could pull their triggers. My Colt bucked up in my hand and the man charging up the low hill at me jerked backward and sideways and went down out of his saddle, but one foot caught in the stirrup. His horse reared up and then began to run, dragging the dead man into the midst of the milling, terrified longhorns.

That's when they broke into a stampede. I didn't have time to watch that, for the second man had swerved and was heading for me. He was a good ways off but was closing fast. I slapped the six-shooter into its holster and grabbed for the Winchester. There was no time to aim. I began pumping shots at the target looking up toward me. He fell clear, dropping like a stone. His horse shied and then ran off, holding his head to one side so he wouldn't step on the trailing reins. The third had seen the two go down and he wheeled around. He was riding like a bat out of hell toward the adobe house, and he was out of range of my rifle.

I ran to my horse just as Joe Bob and Lon and Slocum came swooping down the hill across the valley, working their way toward the terrified cattle. The horse dragging the body was in the middle of them. It was the most horrible thing I have ever seen. Then Joe Bob shot the horse and it went down in a sprawl.

They turned the running longhorns and pointed them toward the pass that led back toward the Rio Grande and Texas, about twenty miles away by the trails they would have to take, though less than half of that as the crow flies.

The Mexican rustlers came boiling out of the adobe house and the tents. They were throwing saddles on their horses and yelling, and then they were off, riding hard. I had to admire the way they handled their horses. Those men could ride.

I gave them a few minutes and then, when they had moved down the valley toward the pass, I rode in well behind them and came down the hill toward the women and children and horses in a high run. If I had hit a prairie dog hole I'd a' been long gone.

I began shooting at the sky, and the women grabbed the children and ran toward the house.

I pulled up my horse and he sat back on his haunches, sliding up toward the corral in a great big cloud of dust. I looped the reins around a rail and tied my pony in a matter of seconds.

I was sure that the rustlers had heard my shots and would be heading back to save their women and kids. I just prayed to God that none of the women had a gun and I could catch Dan before the men got back.

I half flew over the corral fence with my rope in my hand and ran into the scrambling horses. They were to the left of me and to the right. They were running and rearing and kicking and whinnying, and I could hardly see for the dust and confusion. Then the shots began and I realized that the women had rifles and were shooting from the house toward the corral. I got my rope on Dan. It was easy to spot him, for he was a foot taller than any of the rest of the horses.

I walked him to the gate where I had tied my horse and opened it. Thank God that the other horses were between me and the house. Rifles were barking and horses were rearing and plunging and bucking. Several of them were wounded and were screaming as only a horse can.

Dan was back on his hind feet, but I hauled him down. I didn't have time to calm him, and I sure as hell couldn't wait to change saddles there. I could just make out the shape of men riding fast down the valley toward me. Like I'd figured, the Mexican outlaws were headed back.

I untied my pony, mounted, and looped the lead rope around the saddle horn. Then I clapped my spurs into my horse's sides and we were off. I was leaning down low on my pony's neck and he was stretched out, scattering rocks and dust as we skirted through ceniza and greasewood bushes at a full run. Dan was striding easy on his lead rope, keeping up with no trouble. The rifle fire behind me was building up, and every few moments a funny, flat *whap* sound would whip by as a bullet buzzed past my ear.

I pulled up in some boulders and jumped down. Real quick I hauled the saddle off the cow pony and then the bridle, and gave him a slap with the reins. He ran off and I could see the men in the twilight veer and chase him. I reloaded and then got the bridle and saddle on Dan and pulled the cinch up good and tight. We'd have some riding to do. I felt I could get away.

The rustlers saw my pony had been unsaddled, and they

pulled up short and yanked their horses around, spurs raking like you would a bronc, and then they were pounding up the hill after me. By this time I was on Dan and he was going up toward the boulders where I could see a way through to open country. Dan was strong and fresh and climbed with great strong leaps and bounds. But the outlaws had the angle on me. I couldn't make it. It was like they were turning me. I pulled Dan around and headed straight up the steep hill, over rough, rocky land. I only had to touch him with my spurs to feel him surge beneath me. His power gave me confidence. We were going to make it!

Dan lunged up to the top of the hill and I was ready to let him go full out. Then I hauled back in on the reins and Dan reared back. My blood went cold for straight cliffs ran up on three sides. They had herded me into a corner. The only way out was back down into the mouths of the outlaw guns. For a few seconds I knew real panic. I was trapped! They had me! Then I thought, "Well, not without a scrap."

I jumped off Dan and tied him to a scrawny cedar tree. There were seven or eight men bunched up together on horseback, scrambling up the hill. Several pulled their pistols when they saw me, but with their horses lunging forward, driving hard up the hill, there wasn't much chance of my getting hit.

I don't know if they were puzzled about me standing up there in the blood-red sunset that hit the tops of the hills and covered the faces of the cliffs, though it was getting dark in the valley. Everything was happening so fast that they probably didn't think at all, being so mad about my shooting at their women and kids, for they must have thought that was what I had done. They were yelling and cussing in Spanish and were like hunters closing for the kill.

They knew the country and they had headed me into a place with no escape.

I pulled the stick of dynamite out of my saddlebag and opened my knife quick, so as to cut the fuse off real short, just like Culley did when he took me fishing. Then I struck a match and lit it, and in the same instant threw it in a high arc down toward the last men.

The dynamite went off with an explosion that seemed to rock the whole mountain. Several men and horses were thrown left and right. By then I lit a second stick and flung it down toward the men in the lead, who had pulled up short, and the second blast rocked me back on my heels. It covered up the echoes of the first one.

There was a terrible ringing in my ears from the two incredibly loud explosions. Dan was jumping and pulling and I untied him. I kept talking and trying to get close to him while he rolled his eyes and reared back and high-stepped all around me. Finally I was able to get in the saddle and he steadied down. Then I looked down the hill. I could scarcely believe my eyes. There were eight men down. Six were still and two were crawling toward their guns. It was too much for my mind to accept, all the blood and horror, and I froze. The two had their guns up and I felt something seem to snap in me as I made my draw, like my hand was acting on its own. I heard two shots ring out. The two rustlers didn't have a chance. They died on the spot.

I pulled out the Winchester and pumped shells into the horses that were kicking. Then I rode down the hill as far off to one side as I could so I wouldn't have to see what I had done. When I got to the valley I let Dan have his head and he took me in a long, smooth lope, past the house where I heard the women and children screaming and crying.

They never saw me. I slowed Dan to a trot when I got to the pass and then we headed north.

It was daylight when I caught up, and we kept going without stopping. By that night we crossed with what cows and steers we hadn't lost.

When we got back to the ranch I was too tired to sleep, but Joe Bob fixed me a plate of deer meat and frijole beans and a cup of coffee. On the ride back I had forced myself not to think. But now we were home safe. I was bone-tired and my nerve was on the edge of giving way.

They sat there and then Lon said, "We watched the gunfight when the three men came after you, Tom. It was a mighty close call if you ask me. But what on God's green earth happened after that? We heard all this gunfire and explosions like cannons going off. What in hell happened?"

I tried to answer but I couldn't. They could see I couldn't talk about it. I walked out by a tree and for the first time I checked my gun to make sure it was loaded. It was, although I couldn't remember reloading it. It was strange that I hadn't checked it before now. My mind wasn't working right.

When I came back to the house I felt more settled. Joe Bob said, "Here, drink this, boy." He had never called me that before. Maybe he felt fatherly.

I took the cup and from the smell I knew it was whiskey, but I drank it down like medicine. After what had happened nothing in the past quite measured up. I didn't give a hoot in hell for the present or future either.

Joe Bob said, "We heard the explosions. I won't ask how you came to be carrying dynamite. You're a mighty surprising man." He paused a minute. "We heard a lot of shooting before and after the dynamite went off."

Slocum asked, "How many did you get?"

Then I answered, and my voice sounded cold and calm,

though I wasn't. I said, "I got them all. I killed ten men. It wasn't what I had figured on, but that's what happened."

Lon exclaimed, "My God in heaven!" Joe Bob and Slocum didn't look like they could say a thing. Then Lon said, "I don't reckon we'll be having more rustling around here." I allowed that I hoped he was right.

The next day I saddled Bess and got Dan on a lead rope, leaving the packhorse behind. After packing my bedroll and saddlebags with enough provisions to get back to the Clarke ranch, I moved on out. The boys had seemed uneasy around me, like I might go crazy and gun them down or something, but maybe that was just in my mind.

I told them about my promise to Judge Roy Bean about the first colt and thanked them before I left.

CHAPTER 9

It was a nice day though a bit windy. I leaned back in the saddle and took my rope loose with my right hand. Making small loops and roping bushes passed the time for a while as I rode along. It was like I needed to do something so I wouldn't think. There was a despair in me so thick you could cut it with a knife. Yet there was no way to take back what had happened. I knew now how poor my judgment had been. And I couldn't forget the panic I had felt boxed in by those cliffs.

I rode into Langtry and got off my horse at the store. After tying Bess and Dan to the rail, I went inside. Since they had no beer I bought a glass of whiskey and came back out and sat down beside the judge. Several of his hired guns were leaning up against the wall down from where I sat, and I could see them out of the corner of my eye. I told the old scoundrel who claimed to be the law west of Pecos, "The boys will send that colt to you later on."

The judge took a chew off his plug of tobacco and nodded. I suspect he was surprised I had the nerve to come back in town, but to tell the truth I had come in spoiling for trouble. The things that had happened had caused any common sense I ever had to boil over in me, and now I felt like I was so full of meanness that I absolutely didn't give much of a damn what happened. The sickness was in me from the slaughter in Mexico.

The judge said, "I wouldn't have recognized you with that mustache. I do recognize your horses, though."

He saw me eyeing the men down at the end of the porch and he went on, "Don't worry about none of those fellows startin' anything." He looked at me straight in the eye and he said, "We've heard what happened in Mexico."

I wondered how he could have heard, though people said he knew everything that went on for fifty miles around.

He walked over to the edge of the porch to spit, then he rubbed his mouth and sat back down. "They say you're the meanest man in West Texas. I reckon they could add northern Mexico to that."

Feeling a hatred well up in me that I couldn't understand, I paid for my drink and left. I stepped up into the saddle on Bess and then, with Dan following on the lead rope, I headed toward the Pecos River.

That night I took the precaution of camping without a fire. I wouldn't have put it past the judge to have me followed. The next morning I left before dawn, angling east after fording the Pecos, and then riding through the rocky, arid land. The only life I saw was a buzzard a long way off. Finally I got to a crossing on Devils River, where I got off and rested. There was no real reason for it but I felt tired and beat down. I was lower than a lizard's belly. If one had crawled over me, I was thinking, he wouldn't feel a bump. I couldn't help but grin at that. Well, what the hell, I just got back on old Bess and headed north, figuring on going back to Santa Rita by way of Sonora and Eldorado.

When I rode into Santa Rita I didn't expect to be recognized, and I wasn't. For one thing I had a mustache now, and for another it had been two years since I had stepped into Malone's Saloon. After getting the two horses settled in the livery stable I went over to the hotel. I hadn't spent any money in a long time, so as long as I was in town I decided to do it up brown. First I paid for a hot bath. They brought in steaming water and poured it into a big wood tub with iron bands around it. After they left I took off my grimy, salt-stiff clothes and got in. It fair took my breath away. Then I soaked and relaxed so well I blame near drowned. Later I went to my room and stretched out on a sure enough bed. It had been so long since I had done that that I could scarcely remember. The next thing I knew it was pitch-dark. I had dozed off. I got up and went downstairs, after putting on fresh, clean clothes, and ordered a thick T-bone steak, with frijoles and jalapeño peppers and fried potatoes.

The waitress said, "Mister, you act plumb starved to death," and I told her I was close to it, all right. I went back upstairs to my room and got my boots and clothes off and fell in the bed. I made sure my six-gun was handy under the edge of my pillow, and before I knew it I was asleep. I slept so hard it was a job to get waked up. I would try to open my eyes and then give up on it and drop back off. When I finally did come wide awake it was midmorning. I couldn't remember sleeping so late in all my life, or being so rested.

I got some water and shaved. I hadn't seen a good mirror in quite a while, and I looked at the full mustache I had managed to grow. I stood there, looking in the mirror at a dark, tanned face with serious light blue eyes that stared right back at me. I couldn't get over how different I looked with the mustache. It was as though I had put on another ten years. I practiced a few frowns, and then couldn't help but bust out laughing. What I had been feeling wasn't the beginning of a new person with a mean streak a yard wide. Hell, I had just been tuckered out. Well, from now on, I decided, I was going to drift along and be my own self. No more running, no more worrying. Whatever came—well, it could just come.

All of a sudden the anxiety left me. I turned away and the simple decision that I had run enough seemed to make me feel free. It's kind of hard to explain. If anyone wanted to look for Tom English he would be able to find him. I strapped on my six-gun and tied it down. Then I got my bedroll and saddlebags and Winchester and walked down the steps. After settling my account there and at the livery stable I saddled Bess, got my lead rope on Dan, and rode to the Lower Ranch. When I arrived no one but the cook was around. Mr. Field and the boys were out working the stock. After the cook fixed me a slab of beef and some coffee, I asked him to tell Mr. Field that I would be back to see him and left for the Clarke ranch. But by the time I got close I was nervous. I didn't like coming in unannounced. I wasn't expected for another two months. For another thing, I was wondering at the reception I would get from Sally. It had been at the back of my mind for a long time.

I needn't have been so worried. She saw me riding in from a distance and came running to meet me, with her hair flying out behind her. The next thing I knew I was standing on the ground and holding her clear up in the air.

That evening at supper I felt like I was back home, for Mr. Clarke and his wife and Culley and all the rest were acting real happy to see me.

Afterward the men went into the parlor and this time I took a drink along with them. I didn't have to tell them about the trouble. Bad news travels fast. It turned out that the Del Rio newspaper had caught wind of the story and, because it was unusual, the San Antonio paper had carried it too. From there it had spread. It turned out that the Mexican authorities were raising hell about what they called "border warfare." The Del Rio reporter had talked to several people in Villa Acuña, Mexico, who probably didn't know what they were talking about, and also to some in Langtry, Texas, who did. The report was that "the infamous Tom English" had tracked down and killed ten Mexicans who he suspected of rustling, leaving grieving widows and children behind.

After a while I told them just what had happened, and I gave Culley the credit for showing me how to handle dynamite.

To my surprise Mr. Clarke said he would like to talk to me alone, and in a minute the others had left. Then Mr. Clarke poured another drink for himself and for me and looked over his glass at me.

"My daughter, Sally, sets a lot of store by you," he said. "Well," I replied, "I think the world and all of her." We sat there until I couldn't handle the quiet anymore. I said, "I surely do." Mr. Clarke smiled at that and said, "Then I take it your intentions are honorable?"

Now, I'd had a few thoughts that may not have been entirely honorable, although you'll notice I haven't included them in this account, but I hadn't thought through just what my "intentions" were.

"Well, yes, they are. Of course they are," I said. Mr. Clarke said, "That is mighty good news." Then he called out and the entire family came in. They had all been listening, I suppose, for Culley was laughing fit to kill and pretty Sally was completely flustered. I had no idea what Mr. Clarke might say next, so I walked outside and Sally came after me, to the sound of a good many comments. They were fair razzin' us.

We walked out to the corral and old Dan stuck his head over the top rail for me to rub his nose. It's funny how soft a horse's nose is. Sally leaned up against me and before I could stop myself I had asked her to marry me and she said, "Oh, yes."

Now, as an engaged person it ain't proper to discuss the hugging and kissing no more, though you can well imagine the enthusiasm that went into it.

"I dearly love your mustache, Tom, even though it does make you seem so old." She ducked her head. "And it tickles."

"I'll shave it off."

"No, don't do that. I like it. Let's see if I can't get used to it."

There was a good bit of this foolishness along with a considerable amount of sighing and the like.

"I want you to promise me one thing, Tom." She waited until she knew she had my full attention. Then, in a very serious way, almost a tearful one, she said, "I want you to put up your gun for good and all."

When I didn't answer, she said, in such a quiet voice that I could hardly hear her, "I want children, Tom, and I want them to have a daddy around."

Well, that got through to me, so I allowed that I would certainly think about it.

That night I took off the six-gun that Mr. Field had given me. I sat on the bed and took it clear apart. Then I spent the better part of an hour cleaning it and oiling it after I had put it back together. I got some saddle soap and worked on the holster and the cartridge belt, and then I put some neat's-foot oil on the holster.

I was superstitious about that Colt. The idea of being without it made a chill go up my spine and I actually saw goose bumps on my arms.

That night I had the dream of being too slow and looking down the barrel of a .45, and I waked up with a start, with my hand grabbing at my hip. No gun was there, of course, and I was in a sweat. It was mighty hard getting back to sleep.

CHAPTER 10

For the next few days I would wake up with the most peculiar feelings. I would be happy and nervous at the same time. To work off the energy I went out to the corral to help break some mighty raw horses that Mr. Clarke had bought. The things I had learned about bronc riding at the Circle X came in handy, for a few of these horses were rank. There was one in particular named Banjo that had mostly workhorse in him. He was a fine-looking animal, heavy and bigboned with pie plate–sized hooves, but he had a crazy look about him. Then I noticed that he had one brown eye and one blue one. No one had been able to stay on him more than a few seconds, so the cowboys and Mr. Clarke and Culley all came down to watch the proceedings the morning I worked up my nerve to try him. One fellow was earing him down, and he had a bandanna over his eyes, while two others had him choked down with a rope, and Culley and I were trying to get a saddle on him. Out of the corner of my eye I saw a flash of white skirt and knew that Sally had come down to watch. But what with all the hell that Banjo was raising I didn't have a chance to think about it.

The next thing I knew I was in the saddle and had hold of the rope to the hackamore. The choke rope was off and Culley whipped the bandanna away from Banjo's eyes and everyone let go. Then I knew I was in for it. He would twist in midair, then come down stiff-legged, with his head down between his front hooves, and then he would change directions. He would spin and charge and bolt. Every now and then we would bang against the fence, and once he reared up, looking to fall over backward. I hit his head hard with the butt of my quirt, which was loaded with lead. It staggered him, but then he did get mad. I am here to tell you that if ever a horse could scream, it was that Banjo. He must have been not only the orneriest but the loudest horse in kingdom come.

Well, it probably only lasted twenty minutes, give or take a little, though it seemed like half a day. When Banjo would stop, and I'd think he had given in, he would just be taking a deep breath, and then off he would go again. But at last he quit and I got off.

Banjo was bloody, for I had raked him with my spur rowels, from way high in his shoulders down. I was bloody too. My nose was bleeding and there was a little blood coming out of my mouth. My ears were ringing and I hurt all over. All I could do when I got out of the corral was to get down on one knee in front of a horse trough and stick my head down in the water. Then things got a little clearer, but I was still dizzy. All the boys were hooting and hollering. "Damnedest ride I ever *did* see," old Scooter Evans said over and over again. Jim Farr said, "Jesus Christ in the mountains, boy! Where did you learn how to ride?"

After supper that night I went out on the porch. My head hurt and my back hurt and my legs hurt and my rear end hurt. I might as well stop making a list. There wasn't anything that didn't hurt.

Mr. Clarke came out and said, and there was real admiration in his voice, "That was some ride you put on this morning, Tom. I don't know that we'll see the likes of it soon again." I told him that I certainly hoped that *I* never saw the likes of it again. He could tell I was hurting and he was sympathetic. He said, "We'll get Mrs. Clarke to get a couple of hot water bottles for you tonight, and maybe some hot poultices."

We sat together and listened to the locusts whir in the elm and live oak and pecan trees he had planted around the house. Then he said, "Tom, it ain't enough to have quick hands, or to be a natural-born rider. You can get to be a top hand on some ranch, riding like you do, and you might keep on building your reputation with a gun, but where does it all lead? A man needs direction. He needs to think about his future."

I was quiet. I knew he was right, but I had always just taken what came along. To tell the truth, I didn't know how to do anything other than that.

"Tom, I would like you to make something worthwhile out of your life. Jason Field is the oldest friend I've got, and he has a real interest in you. He and I have been talking and we have decided that we are going to offer you a business proposition."

I had no idea what he was talking about. He kept on. "Jason owns ten sections that are long and thin on the north end of the Upper Ranch. This comes to six thousand four hundred acres. It had been in the hands of five different owners and he gradually bought them out, one by one. The land is good, but it has too much mesquite in it. On the other hand, it is on both sides of the North Concho and has real good water. There are big ranchers on both sides of the place that have to bring their herds through this land to water. The ranch is stretched out and it is a considerable distance from one end to the other. It's hard to work, but you could handle it.

"Jason has agreed to take your note for the land, and I have decided to stock the ranch for you with cattle and the horses you'll need. Naturally, I'll take a note too."

I was downright floored. I said after a while, "I can't tell you how much I appreciate this, but I can't accept it."

Now, Mr. Clarke didn't get to be as big a man as he was without being smarter than a whip. He had me half believing that I would be doing him and Mr. Field a favor to make what he called that "little spread" into something.

Sally came out on the porch and said, "Please say yes, Tom." It seemed like she knew all about it. I was so happy about her and all of a sudden having a real direction to go, that I said I would do it, but that I would have to sign a note with full interest for him and Mr. Field, and I couldn't count it as mine until it paid out.

"Of course. That's exactly what we're doing, son. This is good business for all concerned."

I realized that he was helping me because of Sally, and maybe Mr. Field was too, though I was aware that he liked me. But I was bound and determined to make the Lazy E, which I had long ago picked to be my brand if ever I had a chance to use one, into one of the finest ranches of its size in the state of Texas. I guess every cowboy dreams of having his own place someday, though Lord knows that not one in ten thousand gets his wish. It just seemed too good to be true.

Mr. Clarke knew when to leave, and for a while Sally and I sat in the porch swing and courted. Then she said, "I was serious about the gun, Tom." Her voice broke like she was about to cry. "I can't marry a gunfighter. I couldn't stand wondering every day if you'd come home or not." Then she began to cry in earnest. My shirt was getting wet and I fumbled around, rubbing her hair.

"Well, hell, Sally—"

"Tom, please don't curse."

"I'm sorry I said that. It just slipped out." I had been able to handle three quarters of a ton of wild horse, but I sure couldn't handle just over one hundred pounds of little girl. So the upshot of it was that I promised to put the gun away.

That night I wrapped it very carefully in an old shirt and put it in the bottom drawer of the chiffonier in the room that I now considered "mine."

CHAPTER 11

Getting married is considerably more complicated than it sounds like. It seemed there would be no end to the confusion, and I am here to tell you that the week before the wedding I was like a sleepwalker. Sally was just as flustered as I was, so we spent most of the time making calf eyes at each other while her mother did all the work.

Then, all of a sudden, it was done. The honeymoon at the hotel in Santa Rita was behind us and I was slapped in the face with the realization that I had someone who depended on me.

I had signed the notes and we had our own little ranch. The Clarke and the Field cowboys had pitched in and helped with the house. We built it on a rise about a quarter of a mile west of the Concho in the midst of a stand of live oak trees. A finish carpenter from Santa Rita had done the interior and the cabinet work, and then he and I painted some parts of it and stained the rest. While it was small, it seemed to my eye to be the very nicest house I had ever seen. And Sally was beside herself about it. We painted the walls of her kitchen a gray blue that she mixed for us, and did the shutters and cabinets and trim in white.

We didn't have much furniture, but we had enough to do for the time, and just before the wedding it was ready.

Mr. Clarke helped me pick out the breeding stock for the ranch. I went along with his advice and took only the chunky white-faced Herefords.

We cut about twenty mares from his horses with care. This was a special joy for me for I have always loved horses. Mr. Clarke was real enthusiastic about this and it wasn't until our wedding day that I found out why. He gave us his fine stallion, Dan, as our wedding present.

The whole Clarke family had been in on this surprise and they were all standing around to watch my face when they brought Dan up and presented him to me. I was speechless. Then the fun began. Culley said that it looked like I was more excited about getting Dan than I was about marrying Sally, and then the others picked up on it. But it was all in fun.

Well, all of this was part of the confusion. But the really important thing was Sally. Even now, thinking back on it, I choke up, for no man has ever loved a woman like I loved her. I could not then, and still can't, believe my good luck.

Then, all of a sudden, there we were, acting like we were grown-ups, in our own house. It seemed to me to be too good to last. You worry about things like that when times are good. You fret about what some have called "laws of compensation." I don't set store by any such laws. But the funny feeling was there. Maybe that is why I got so terribly upset when, out of a clear blue sky, Sally took sick.

At first it wasn't much, but each day she felt worse. She couldn't seem to shake it off. After a week had passed and there was no sign of improvement, I rode to Santa Rita for the doctor. It was a hard ride, almost thirty miles, and he had to come on horseback, for after you got to our ranch there were trails but no roads good enough for his buggy.

It was almost dark the second day when we got back. Sally was a brave girl but I knew she was worried about herself. She had never had a day's sickness before.

Old Doc Starret was stiff as a post from riding all day, and he creaked around the house complaining to beat the band, just like he had done ever since I had insisted that he come out to the ranch. Sally was sure in no shape for me to take her in to see him.

Well, it wasn't any time at all before I heard the doctor fuming and fussing. He went out on the gallery that went around the house and sat down on the porch steps and lit his pipe. His face was red and he cussed for a good five minutes. Then he turned to me and began to laugh.

"I'm certainly glad I came out here to save Sally's life. By God, if I had been sixty years later it would almost certainly have been too late. However, I expect she will pull through this present malady." Then he began cussing and laughing both at the same time.

He pulled himself up and went into the house and I followed him into the kitchen with what Sally said later was a baffled look on my face. She was blushing and smiling when Doc said, "And the next time your wife gets in the family way you take her over to her mother and don't bother me about it until it's time for the baby to be delivered."

I sat down at the kitchen table and for no good reason I felt like crying like a little kid, but of course I didn't. So, after petting Sally and, I expect, babbling a good bit, I opened the bottle of bourbon Culley had given me before our wedding, and I poured a drink out for the doctor, and a real stiff one for me.

That night I got drunk for the first and last time. When I waked up Sally was tending to me, and she said, "I feel like a perfect fool, and you acted like one."

After that I went to work in earnest. I hired two good hands to help out, and we built a corral, some pens, a barn, and a shed for supplies. Then we built a bunkhouse and another shed for our saddles and bridles and gear. I hired three Mexican cowboys and, since one of them, a fine older man named Benito, spoke some English, we didn't have any trouble letting them know what had to be done.

In a few months we had cleared the way for a road that we needed so it connected with the road through the other ranches that meandered around until it got to Santa Rita. When it came time for the baby to come, our plan was to use our new wagon and take Sally to her mother's house, and then send for Doc Starret to come out to help her.

The six-gun had been put away and I had given up practicing. Once in a while my bad dream woke me up, but with Sally there next to me I could forget all about it. After a while the dream stopped. I reckon all the rest of my worries crowded it out. From not really thinking beyond what I might do the next day, I had reached the point where I was damn near a nervous wreck. The heavy debts to Mr. Clarke for the stock and Mr. Field for the ranch bothered me, but on top of that I owed the First National Bank in Santa Rita close to four thousand dollars. Mr. Clarke had gone on my note when this loan had been made. He had said, "Now, Tom, it takes money to make money. A man needs a stake. If I ain't worried, why should you be?" Well, I just was, that's all.

It wasn't long after that when things started looking up. Nearly all the mares were in foal, and Mr. Clarke's big red herd bull, which he had loaned me, Prince Hal was his name, was seeing to it that the cows would bear calves. One evening I came home to find Sally bustling around getting supper ready. She was already heavy with the child, and I said, "I spend all day with pregnant mares and cows and then come home to a pregnant wife."

She came over for me to hug on her, saying, "Now, Tom," like she was mad, but she wasn't. She was so proud of what she was doing that it was all she could think about. She would say, in a small, wondering voice, "There is a little human being growing inside of me!" We couldn't get over the marvel of it.

At night Benito would play his guitar and sing Mexican songs, and because we had worked hard all day we would be tired and would lean back and listen. What I'm trying to explain, I guess, is that, with all the worry and all the work, it was the best of times. So many things were being created.

When Sally's time was near I took her to her mother's house. That same night, or rather very early the next morning, Agnes called me and said I had better fetch Doc Starret. I saddled Dan, for I had brought him along for this very occasion. It was along about 4 A.M. and Dan settled into his long, smooth trot. He could hold that gait all day, and the miles moved under us. By noon I was in town and Doc Starret sent out word to hitch his two horses, a fine bay team he was right proud of, to his buggy. He rolled out of town after I told him that I was going to catch my wind, but that I would be along directly. I put Dan at the livery stable and unsaddled him. After rubbing him down good I got him water and some oats and hay.

While he was attending to his feed I walked over to the Main Street Bar and had a couple of drinks. A tall kid came in, looking right at me, and I watched him in the mirror. He was jumpy. Suddenly I had an idea of what was going to happen.

He edged up behind me and I half turned just as he was pulling his six-gun. I swung as hard as I could with the whiskey bottle and it shattered to smithereens across his forehead before his gun had even cleared its scabbard. He went down hard, and blood flew all over the place. Then he tried to sit up just as I smashed a chair into his right shoulder and arm. I could feel something snap. It was all over in a matter of seconds.

The bartender hollered for someone to go get the doc, but I knew he had already left town and told him so. He looked at me in a peculiar way and began trying to stop the bleeding. He wrapped some dishrags as tight as he could around the kid's head.

The bartender had a deep, gruff voice and he was muttering to me, "I seen him try to jump you from behind. He was going for his gun, although he could see you wasn't armed. I can't say I blame you for what happened. On the other hand, that there chair wasn't necessary. Hell, he's more dead than alive."

I answered, "He'll make it, I reckon. I just didn't want him trying to gun me anytime soon."

The bartender said, "He ain't going to use that right arm for a mighty long time, if he ever uses it."

Then he said, "Mr. English, please don't take offense, but I would be much obliged if you'd drink elsewheres in the future. It seems like trouble follows you."

I didn't know what to say to that, so I paid for the two drinks and walked out.

It was a sunny day, just past noon, and I stood for a spell. Several people edged around me, and I could see folks whispering to each other, nervous like, and looking at me. One old fellow was cackling, "That there Tom English would just as soon kill a man as look at him. He'll kill you with his gun or he'll kill you with his bare hands." He hooted like this was some kind of big joke, and the people with him told him to hush up, that I could hear him.

I went to the livery stable and washed the blood off my hands and clothes, as best I could. I was nineteen years old and I had killed fifteen men and crippled up another. I felt a cold rage well up. I hadn't looked for this trouble today. This was supposed to be one of the happiest days of my life. But there was a bitter taste in my mouth as I saddled

Dan and started toward the Clarke ranch. When I got out of town, away from all of the people, when I got where there was just Dan and me moving through the mesquite trees, heading northwest, the rage passed on.

I felt gooseflesh ripple as I rode along. If the kid had been more experienced, if he had stood ten feet away, I wouldn't have had a chance. Instead of riding back to Sally I would be dead. But then I forgot about that and thought just of Sally and the new baby.

CHAPTER 12

I don't want it to sound like bragging but Rebecca was the prettiest baby girl that was ever born. By the time she was three years old she was even prettier. Doc Starret had worked with Sally for fourteen hours before he delivered Rebecca, and he explained to me that Sally would never be able to have another child. But it didn't matter for we had this golden girl with her mother's dark brown eyes and curly reddish brown hair. It doesn't do to try to describe her. It was enough for me to sit and watch her.

In that three years the Lazy E had done a lot better than I would have expected. The bank debt was paid and so was the Clarke note for my stock. Over half the Field note for the land was paid and it looked like in two more years the rest would be retired.

They say one of the only things you can depend on is change, and I reckon that is correct. I suppose that if I ever have three good years in a row again I'll get leery. Come to think about it, there is something else dependable. I'm not talking about death and taxes. I'm talking about drought in West Texas. The unusual thing is when there *isn't* a drought there.

We had been through one of those rare periods of regular rainfall that people would like to think of as normal. Well, we got back to what was truly normal the year that Rebecca was two. It rained just at nine inches that year, but eight of that was in April. It all fell at once and the

Concho flooded and ran over its banks. We had a big time roping stock that would get carried off by the water. It made me feel like a kid again. We lost some cattle and instead of crying about it I was out having a good time.

That was sure the last fun we had that year. It rained a few sprinkles here and there the rest of the year, and that was all. It would get cloudy out in the west, where our rain comes from as a general rule, and we would get our hopes up and get excited. The lightning would flicker and we would hear the promises that the long rumbles of thunder made, but then nothing would happen.

The next year it didn't seem like it rained at all. Even the mesquite trees and the prickly pear began to die, and the old-timers had only known that to happen once before. A mesquite tree puts out roots that spread far out in all directions. Just try to pull up a young mesquite, say one about three feet tall. They are skinny and wispy at that height and it looks easy, but it can't be done. It already has its roots too far out and too far down. Hell, in that dry country, it has to do that to get the moisture to live; as for the prickly pear, who would think it would get too dry for cactus? So when they began to die we knew we were in bad trouble. The cattle would miss eating mesquite leaves and beans, for the grass was long gone. The earth was as dry as talcum powder.

I had hired a fair-sized crew of Mexican workers, and with Benito acting now as foreman and giving the orders, we burned the spines off the prickly pear we had left. These men, the ones everybody called pear grubbers, for they dug up the prickly pear with picks and shovels, were a hard-working lot, and asked little pay so long as they had plenty of frijoles and an occasional Spanish goat or kid. The money they earned they sent home to Old Mexico. You had to respect them.

While it lasted the prickly pear made good feed. It surprised me that the other ranchers didn't use it more. But most of them were in the habit of accepting trouble when it came along, and maybe they didn't think it seemly to fight back. On the other hand they may have been so depressed that it didn't appear worthwhile to try to keep the cattle alive a little longer when it looked like they were going to die anyway.

The other real worry was that the Concho was down to a trickle. There were some holes of water here and there, but there sure wasn't enough to spare.

There has been many a man who has damned me through the years for what I did. There are some who swore to kill me, and a few tried. But I did what had to be done. I had some money saved and I ordered the long heavy spools of barbed wire, what all of us call "bob wire," to be sent out by wagons all the way from San Antonio. I had to hire extra Mexicans and buy some wagons and teams to handle all of it, together with the hammers and staples and axes we would need. We had to buy quite a few post-hole diggers and wire stretchers too. I had decided to fence the Lazy E.

In those days no one had fenced anything at all except maybe for a small pasture, a trap we called it, where we would keep some horses, or stock that needed doctoring. The Lazy E was ten sections, ten square miles, and it was long and thin on both sides of the North Concho. The practice had been for the big ranchers to leave their stock loose and it would naturally water at the Concho, and eat my grass while they were at it. When there was plenty of grass and weeds it didn't matter as much. My cattle would mix with theirs, and graze on their land more than mine, and water back at our place. But now there wasn't enough water to go around.

It took months to get the fence up. We used mesquite limbs for posts, which we would chop with axes. Then we had to dig postholes. I had gotten a surveyor and he tagged trees and put down stakes along our property line, so we knew exactly where the fence was to go.

During this time we had some visitors who gave us hell for what we were doing, but it didn't really dawn on them what was about to happen.

When the fence was finally up we had a big roundup and sorted out our stock of cattle and horses, and we got them inside the Lazy E's fences.

At first they tried cutting the fence to get to the river. I had figured it might come to that and I had bought Winchesters for Benito's men. In the three years I had worked with Benito I had come to respect him, and over a period of time I got to the place where I could talk enough Spanish to get along. As a matter of fact, since I talked it practically all day long with the cowboys, I had gotten pretty damn good at it, if I do say so myself. Another thing that developed was that some of our pear grubbers made fine cowboys. They had been starved out of Mexico and had come across the Rio Grande on foot, willing to take on any kind of work at all. Some had worked as vaqueros in their own country before, and they all could ride. They were terribly proud to have horses and saddles. I got them boots and spurs and after a time I armed them.

We had fence riders with Winchesters from then on clear around the borders of the Lazy E. Benito sent to Piedras Negras in Mexico, across from Eagle Pass, Texas, for more help to replace some of our men who quit. It's not everybody who has the stomach for trouble, and the men could smell it coming. Benito had kinfolk in Piedras Negras and he claimed that some were pretty fair hands with guns. We supplied the new men with rifles and we set up an informal school where I worked with new and old alike on marksmanship. It got to be a kind of competition, and every once in a while we would set up targets and I'd offer a kid goat to the winner. There would be a big feast of baked cabrito and frijoles afterward, so in a way everyone was a winner. There was usually horseplay and laughter but we all knew this was in dead earnest.

Three different times neighboring ranchers rode in unarmed, escorted by Lazy E vaqueros. They came to try to talk sense to me, as they put it. Well, either my stock would have water and live, or if we took down the fences and all the cattle came to the Concho, then my cattle and everyone else's would die. That's the sense of it as I saw it.

The thing that hurt me was that Mr. Field and Mr. Clarke acted like they sympathized with their neighbors. They never said it in so many words. They declared that it was my business, but I could sense what they felt. My two gringo cowhands quit, so it boiled down to just me and my Mexican cowboys against a large number of very angry folks. I had sure taken up the role of the village villain. I never had felt quite as alone. It was lucky I had Sally and, of course, Rebecca.

The showdown came, as I had figured it would, from John Dawson. He and twenty heavily armed men sent word for me to come to a place called Three Points on the southwest side of the Lazy E. It was called that because it was where the Clarke and Dawson and English ranches came together. There was a property line stake under a big live oak tree there.

Sally watched while I got out my six-gun and filled the cartridge belt with bullets. I filled the cylinder with six .45-caliber cartridges and snapped it into place. She began to cry when I buckled it on and tied it down, and she took Rebecca off and closed the door behind her.

I got my Winchester and then saddled Bess. I had shot with pistols and rifles while riding Bess so often that she was accustomed to gunfire. She would flinch, but there was no going haywire when a shot went off the way you would expect with most cowponies. It's true I hadn't touched a handgun in years, but I still had done my share of hunting, and I always rode Bess at those times.

Benito and his eleven men and I looked like we were ready to start the War Between the States all over again when we got mounted. Every man jack had a six-gun in his holster and was carrying a Winchester in his hand or, if he had one, in a boot mounted on his saddle. Benito passed around some bottles of tequila, looking at me out of the corner of his eye to see if I minded, which I didn't.

Then we set off in a slow lope for Three Points. Before we got there we stopped and talked, and I told them what to do. Then we rode on at a walk. We were saving our horses' strength. We were also putting off for as long as we could what was going to happen.

We saw Big John Dawson and his men lined up at our fence. There was a milling herd of his cattle being held behind him. Two men were on foot with wire cutters and they were cutting wire and taking down the fence as fast as they could. There were three or four hands back with the herd and, as I had heard, there were close to twenty men with Dawson. It looked like they were as well armed as we were.

We rode up to our side of where the fence had been and faced them. I was in the center, face to face with John Dawson. I had my Winchester across my saddle horn. Next to Dawson was a thin young man with a pale face. Under his hat you could see a terrible scar that went from his forehead clear around to above his ear. His right arm was peculiarly bent and stiff and I saw that he wore his gun on his left side. Then I recognized him. It was the kid who had tried to gun me down three years before in the Main Street Bar in Santa Rita.

The kid's eyes were hard as he watched me. He let his left hand fall down beside the butt of his six-gun. I turned Bess slowly to the right so that the muzzle of my rifle moved toward him. He was looking in my eyes and I was looking in his. The tension began to build up and it seemed like something had to explode. Both sides were scared, for the bluff had been called and we were seconds away from what could be the bloodiest day in many a long while.

John Dawson said, "English, my cattle are going to the Concho. You got no right to fence off water. That river serves this whole part of West Texas and you damn well know it."

I said, "Tell those men to stop cutting my fence."

Well, it struck both of us, I reckon, that this wasn't the kind of talk to cause peace to break out. So Dawson said, "Be reasonable, Tom. All we want is to water our cattle. There ain't no grass, so we can't tromp it down. We'll stay with the herd and move them right back off of your property when they have had water."

Then I said, "I'm sorry, Mr. Dawson, but the Concho is almost dry. If there were water enough I'd be happy to oblige you. There just ain't enough."

Dawson looked hard at me and then he said, "I was afraid it would come to this. Everyone knows your reputation, but we have more guns. And this here"—he jerked his head toward the scarred kid with the stiff right arm—"is Steve Epley. He is building a reputation, too. Some say there's no man fast enough to take him. I expect you recognize him. He's our equalizer. He tells me, by the way, that he has a special reason to be looking for you."

I had been watching Epley and he had been keeping his

eyes on me during most of this conversation. Just as Dawson's voice stopped the kid's left hand flashed. He was God-damned fast, I'll say that for him, but he wasn't faster than a Winchester bullet. I blew him clear out of his saddle. One instant he had been sitting on his horse and the next he was flat on his face on the ground, and there was a hole right in the center of his back where the rifle bullet came out that was big enough to put your fist into. There was blood all over the place.

The cowboys on both sides of the fence froze for a second, the second I needed, then Epley's horse reared and kicked and ran off, while I drew my six-gun with my right hand, having switched the rifle to my left. I waved the Winchester over the men on my left and leveled the six-gun at Big John Dawson. It was pointed right between his eyes, and I said, "One move from any one of you and Dawson's head will be blown clear off, and I'll kill at least four of you. You know me, and you know I speak the truth."

Then I said, "Drop your rifles." First one and then another did what I said. I could hear them clatter as they hit the ground. In a minute they had dropped their rifles, and then I had them unbuckle their six-guns and drop them on the ground too.

Dawson's face was drained, it was deathly pale. Then the most unbelievable thing happened. He grabbed his chest and got very red in the face, and his eyes stared out, and he slumped forward. He slid off and fell with a heavy thud on the ground. Several of his men jumped down and ran to him. They knelt beside him and then slowly looked up at me. One of them said, and his voice was almost choked, "He's dead! My God, he's dead!" Then he stared at me and said, "You'll regret this to the end of your days."

CHAPTER 13

Since the time I was just a kid I've hunted. It's born in me, I reckon. I can remember so clearly creeping up on doves. That may not sound like it's sporting, but when you have a single-shot .410-gauge shotgun and you are after supper, that's the best way. Especially when you're seven or eight years old. I was able to be totally still, lying in the tall grass and weeds, and then I would move with such care that they usually didn't see me. More than once I got an angle where I got two with one shot, but that was just luck.

After my ma and dad died I lived with my grandmother, just the two of us. She got a real kick out of those doves I would bring in, I can tell you.

I don't know what made me think about that. I suppose it's because I always considered myself as a hunter and now the tables were turned. People were out to hunt *me* and I didn't like it a damned bit.

They were all around us. I slipped out every now and then and looked things over, and with each day they were getting more men. The Harris outfit to the east was armed, but it was nothing at all like the Dawsons to the west. It struck me that we were in for it.

They were laying back, just out of range, but they were there, camped on the borders of the Lazy E. Two nights after the showdown at Three Points a shot came through the window and hit a kerosene lamp. Sally had been sitting by it in a rocker with Rebecca in her lap. We got the fire out quick enough, but Rebecca was terrified and she kept crying.

Benito and the men had spread out quick, but they didn't find whoever had done it. Somehow a man, or a small group, had slipped past our lookouts.

I was fit to be tied. First the red rage swelled up and then the familiar ice cold madness took its place. Sally tried to talk to me but I couldn't answer.

"What can we do, Tom?

"Why don't you answer me, Tom?"

I was so tied up in knots I simply wasn't able to speak. Sally said, "Don't do anything foolish. Let's go home to Mama."

I couldn't do that. Hell, this was home, and I wasn't going to get run out. But I took Sally and Rebecca to her daddy's place that night in the darkness. I put Sally and Rebecca on Dan, and I rode Bess. We got to the Clarke ranch house just at dawn.

Mr. Clarke sat, drinking coffee, and he said, "The Dawsons are fine people, at least John was. I knew him well. He was a good friend of mine." Then he said, "For that matter I've always got along right well with the Harrises." He shook his head. "This here thing has got clear out of hand. It is an outrage that someone shot into your house. Your story about the fire, with Rebecca crying and Sally helping you beat out the flames, enrages me. But it could have been some wild kid they hired who took it into his head to scare you. I can't think any of the Harris or Dawson people had anything to do with it." His face darkened. "Of course, if one of them did . . ." and his voice trailed off. The threat was there even though it was left unspoken.

Mr. Clarke cleared his voice, for he didn't want to show how strongly he was affected. "That's how I read it, anyway." He said, "Even so, Tom, you started this thing and now you're going to have to face the consequences. One thing is certain, we're on the edge of a real range war, like the one in New Mexico. Gunslingers are arriving every day offering their services and they are being hired. Do you have an answer for it?"

I had to answer, "No, sir, I sure as hell don't." That, now I think about it, was close to being my sole contribution to the conversation. I hope he didn't get mad at me for not talking much. But after a while I kissed Sally and Rebecca and went back home. It was open along the Concho from the Clarke ranch through the Field Upper Ranch to the Lazy E. The danger lay west and east.

When I got back I found Benito in a savage mood. Two of his men had been killed the night before while I was taking Sally and the little one out. Benito and our boys had been ambushed by a good-sized group of men, he wasn't exactly sure how many there were, but they were on our property. Maybe they were the same ones who had put a shot into my living room. Whoever they were, they didn't waste time talking. They opened fire and two of our men, Benito's nephew Marcos and a new boy named Antonio, were dead.

Benito had already sent another relative who was on our payroll, a wild-riding vaquero named Miguel, to Piedras Negras for more help. His kinfolk there were to search out and send to us some men who knew guns, even if they had to go clear to the Durango country to find them. Benito said, speaking in Spanish, words to the effect that "only hard men live in Durango. When those men come here we will take satisfaction." Then he snarled, "*Venganza!*" Well, that is certainly the longest statement Benito had made in the three years I had known him. He wasn't much for talking, but it was clear to me that he was ready to take trouble with him right across our fence to the gunmen waiting out there.

I didn't say much, and that night I went to bed early, after explaining my plan to Benito. Things were moving too fast and if I didn't act now, they would go clear out of control.

I waked up about one o'clock in the morning. If I set my mind to getting up it will wake me damn near every time. Dan had been left at the Clarkes' for safekeeping, so I saddled Bess and went out whistling the signal, a soft whip-poorwill birdcall, so that the guards wouldn't shoot me by mistake. I know where they were stationed and I worked my way through the Lazy E from lookout to lookout. One of my first worries, as I rode west in the darkness, was not to get shot by one of my own men.

I had to cut the wire in the fence to get through to the Dawson ranch. There was just three strands but the wire cutter made a loud *ping* as each one was cut. I was on edge and felt sure each time that the noise had betrayed my position. I waited, down on one knee by the fence, but no one came, so I realized it was simply my imagination.

There was a half moon and I rode northwest by its pale light along the edge of a line of mesquite trees. Old Bess was almost tiptoeing, it seemed to me, with her head up and her ears cocked forward. I had been on many a deer hunt on her, leaning a little forward in the saddle with the Winchester in my right hand, and I suppose she thought we were out on another hunt. In a way we were. I felt a jolt of excitement run through me. It was good not to be holed up, waiting. Now it was their turn to look out.

I could barely make out the trail, but I had ridden this way a few times before and I had a general idea as to where I was going. After a short while I heard the wind clank a few pans on a chuck wagon down in a flat below me on my right, so I made a wide loop left to miss the camp. As I rode down the gentle slope I looked back and could see the silhouette of a cowboy on guard, half asleep and hunched over on his horse.

A few miles farther on I saw a small campfire. I tied Bess and went as close as I dared. Two men were making coffee and complaining. I couldn't hear what they were saying, but from the tone of voice it was some bellyaching about pay or hours or food or all three put together. The same old cowboy lament. It was hard to think that such familiar sounds were coming from people who in all likelihood would shoot me on sight. I went back to Bess and mounted. We made a circle around them like I had done with the first group before.

Less than an hour later I came up to the Dawson ranch headquarters. I tied Bess to a tree limb about two hundred yards or more from the big house that was in front of the barns and pens, and I put the Winchester in the boot on the saddle. Then I kind of ghosted along, from tree to tree, around toward the back of the house. I could see three men standing guard, and maybe there were more. I waited for what seemed an eternity, though it probably wasn't ten or fifteen minutes, until they all happened to walk around together to the front. I suppose they were bored and were talking to each other. It was time to make my move so I made a run to the fence that surrounded the house and climbed over it. It was a white picket fence, put there I suppose to protect the yard from the livestock. There were bushes and a few flowers planted just inside it and I lay down in them to catch my breath. I raised my head, and, not seeing anybody, I got up and ran to the back door. It was a screen door that gave onto a big screened porch. By the moonlight I could just make out a long trestle table with benches inside. It was probably where they fed the hired hands. More than likely there was a formal dining room for the family somewhere else.

I took out my pocket knife and cut the screen. Then I reached through and took the hook off the latch. Funny that people feel secure when they latch a screen door.

I walked inside and decided my best bet would be to get people to come to me. No use getting my fool head blown off wandering into folks' bedrooms. I went into the kitchen and clattered around until I found a kerosene lamp, which I lit. I found the usual pot of frijole beans shoved to the back of the iron stove where the coals would keep it heated up all the time but not boiling, along with a black coffee-pot. I pulled down an old blue enameled tin cup with some of the enamel knocked off the side so that dark metal showed through. Then I got a plate and a fork and a ladle, which I used to get a few frijoles and some salt pork out of the iron pot.

I put the lamp on the table and then brought my plate and cup of coffee and ate for a spell. Still no one came out. Damn! After being so quiet and cautious for hours I was wondering if I was up against a bunch of deaf people. There were several reasons for my visit, but one of them was to startle them, to let them know that they could be on the receiving end of a night attack regardless of how many guards they might stake out.

I put up the plate and clattered around a bit. Still nothing happened. Then I spoke out, not too loud for I didn't want the guards outside to hear me, and I called, "Anybody home?" Now, this is a most peculiar thing to have to say, but after the hours of silence the sound of my own voice like to have scared the hell out of me.

It was at that moment that I heard the sound of footsteps. Two sets of bootsteps were coming down a long hall toward me and I heard one man say, "Earl, I'm telling you I heard something going on back toward the kitchen."

I moved into a dark corner and they walked in, one with a pistol and the other bare-handed. I said, "Drop that gun or you're dead." He was a quick thinker for the gun dropped on the wood floor right then and there. The taller man, the one who had dropped the gun, asked, "Who are you? What are you doing in our house? What do you want?" If I hadn't stopped him I believe he would have been able to keep on asking questions indefinitely.

I edged into the light with my six-gun in my hand and said, "I'm Tom English and I've come to see you." Both men jumped a little. Maybe I looked as crazy as I felt. I said, "I reckon you're Earl and Billy Dawson."

The younger one, Billy, said, "You killed our pa, damn you."

I looked at him and asked, "Who else is in the house?" and Earl said, "Just our wives and the kids and Ma."

There was a long, tense time with no one saying a word, then, while they glared at me, I said, "Your pa had some kind of heart attack, which you know about. He set up that showdown at Three Points, not me. And I shot his gunfighter only when he made the first move."

"Your fence killed Pa."

"My fence didn't do no such thing." I had come over to scare hell out of them and they were threatening me. I didn't feel that things were going the way I had planned. I looked real fierce and pointed my gun at them. "Now look here—" I began. At that minute a young woman with black hair hanging loose down her back to her waist came in and rushed right up to me.

"Don't you dare point that thing at Billy!"

"Stand back, ma'am."

"I'll do no such of a thing!"

Just then Billy made a run for the door and I had to fire a shot right in front of him, splintering a big hole in the wood floor. The explosion made a roar in the closed room that made our ears ring. Of course the guards would have heard it. The three people in the room with me were petrified. The shot had proved to be a lot more effective than conversation.

I grabbed Billy and threw him back toward the others, then I went to the door that opened out onto the screened porch and hollered, "It's all right, boys. My damn gun just went off while I was cleaning it."

Off to one side I heard a relieved man, one of the guards, say, "Jesus Christ! You scared the life out of us. You sure you're okay?"

"You bet. Everything is fine."

Lights must have come on in the bunkhouse because I heard the man yelling, "There ain't no problem. Billy's gun just went off when he was cleaning it." There were sounds of distant laughter and then silence.

I turned to the people with me in the kitchen. They were scared now. Earl said, finally, "You bluffed us and you fooled our guards. Now, you've come in here and taken our food and terrified our women." As he spoke another young woman came in and went to him in a rush when she saw me with the gun. Earl broke off and held her. She said to him, "Your ma has all the children." She stared at me, a pale, pretty woman in her late twenties, with large, dark frightened eyes.

I said, "I have come at night to see you because that's the only way I can. I never could make it in the daytime."

"That's fer damn sure," Billy confirmed.

Then I said, "And as for scaring folks, some of your men shot into my home last night and nearly killed my wife and daughter." They saw how mad I was. I said in just over a whisper, "Two of my men were killed from ambush. It had to be your men who bushwhacked them."

"It was none of our doing. It must have been Harris's men."

"If that's the case, why do you have all the guards out? You must have known I'd come over." I fought to keep from losing control of myself, for I could feel a fury straining inside of me. Holding my voice down, for it had risen, I said, "Well, I can't say who did it. Maybe your men, or maybe Harris's. But be that as it may, I think we should see if there is some way out of this that is more sensible than shooting each other."

Earl asked, "What did you have in mind?" But just then Billy began raving about how I had killed his pa and that I would have to kill him too. He made a run at me with his wife holding on to his arm, which tends to slow a man down, and I rapped him up on the side of the head with the barrel of my Colt. He spun down and banged into the floor.

"I'm sorry I had to do that."

But Earl was mad now so I could tell he wasn't going to talk sense. He called me a few fairly old-fashioned names and asked if I would give him a chance at his six-gun, and I said I wouldn't.

Billy was moaning so I told the women to tend to him, which they did. Then I said, "Earl, there's going to be nothing but bad blood between us from now on. I've got the legal right to fence my property, as you must know. Without the Concho your place is worthless, but I'll give you a fair price for it."

He looked up at me and if there was ever pure hate in a man's eyes I saw it in his. He said, and his voice was hoarse and quivering, "I'll see you in hell first. We might sell the place—we need to sell it—but by God it'll never be to you."

I said, "All right, Earl. I'm sorry I broke in here, but I had to talk to you. And I'm sorry I had to hit your brother."

Then he said, "How do you reckon you're going to get out of here? There are armed men around this house, and a bunkhouse close by with more of my boys. Some are real gunhands who just hired on."

I answered, "I'll get out real easy, Earl. I'm going out to my horse with your wife or with you."

He hesitated for just a minute, and then he said, "Well, you'll go with me."

"Only if you do exactly as I say."

He nodded and I had him tie one end of a long dish towel around one wrist. He looked puzzled, and then I had him lie facedown on the floor with both hands behind him. Then he understood. Billy was sitting up, holding his head in his hands and didn't appear to be a threat. I holstered my pistol and in seconds I had lashed Earl's wrists together behind his back. I helped him get up and we walked from the kitchen and on out the back way. By then I had my six-gun out again.

One of the cowboys who were standing guard came up and I said, "I'm Tom English and I have a .45 on your boss's spine. If you make a sudden move I'll kill him and you too. Do you understand?"

His jaw was hanging open and all he could do was nod up and down, which he did with surprising energy. It was clear that he understood.

"Unbuckle your gunbelt." After he had done this I walked the two of them out to the tree where Bess was tied. I mounted and turned to them with a half smile. "Now it's your turn. You can do your damnedest." I headed off in a lope that turned into a dead run.

I had started straight back for the Lazy E and behind me were shouts and hollering and a few gunshots. The men on guard and the camps of men between me and the Lazy E would be well alerted by now and would be on the lookout. The cowhands and gunmen in the bunkhouse behind me would be in quick pursuit. I swung Bess around to the south, off to my right, and dropped back into a lope. After a bit we slowed to Bess's traveling gait, an easy long trot, and we stayed on our trail to the south. All the while I heard gunfire behind me and toward the Lazy E.

I had warned Benito to have his men posted and I felt sure he could hold off anybody who tried to come in. I didn't believe they had the strength or the foolishness to go after armed men in place at night. Especially in the other man's territory where he knows it and they don't. People are generally very predictable about things like that. Sure enough, the gunfire died down. But I kept on going. I had a new plan and I would need Mr. Clarke or Mr. Field to help me.

CHAPTER 14

It was dawn again when I got to the Clarke ranch, just as it had been the day before. Mr. Clarke looked at me as though he could scarcely believe his eyes, and he said, "Hell, boy, don't you ever sleep?"

After my reunion with Sally and Rebecca, and a big breakfast of stirred eggs and thick toast and salty slabs of bacon with the rind still on it, served with cup after cup of thick, black, hot coffee, I felt better.

I told the story of all that had happened since I had seen them last, and I said, "Mr. Clarke, the Dawsons know their ranch depends too much on the Concho and they want to sell out to anyone but me. I'm pretty sure they'll take a note with fair interest in payment, and the price per acre should be around one dollar. I expect they would accept that offer from you."

He answered, "The day will come when folks would say I stole their land. I wouldn't be comfortable with it."

"Well, it sure beats bloodshed, and besides, I need it. I'll buy it from you at the same price and on the same terms. Any future criticism will fall on my shoulders. As far as being fair goes, they can take that note for collateral and go farther west, maybe out toward Marfa, where there is good grass most of the time. They can buy a ranch there for around the same price they would be getting, and they would be a hell of a lot better off. From my standpoint this will put me in a position to have a better ranch for my family. I'd like to build something for Rebecca."

He shook his head and went out on the porch but, as I had thought he would, he agreed to do it. He was crazy about that granddaughter. He said he would send word for the two Dawson boys to come over to see him in the next day or two, that he had an interesting proposition for them.

While we were talking I saw two men on horseback top the hill and head down toward us. Mr. Clarke saw my eyes and he turned around to study the approaching horsemen. "Appears to be the marshal, Ben Jordan, and Jason Field is with him," he said.

I had a strange feeling just then, though I don't know why. I guess it was that I hadn't slept much and I was on edge. We walked out to the gate to wait for them.

Later, drinking coffee in the dining room, Mr. Clarke said, "You men must have started mighty early to get here at this hour."

Jason Field said, "We did get up before cock crow. It was just at four when we were saddled and on our way. We were figuring on getting you to go with us, and riding on up to the Lazy E to talk turkey to our young friend here." He wasn't smiling as he nodded his head at me.

Ben Jordan's eyes bored a hole in me. He said, "I understand you have started a range war, is that right?"

"It's not a war yet. I think we can head it off. Earl Dawson has a cool head and in my opinion there is a way to settle the problem." Hurriedly I told them of my talk with the Dawsons the night before and of the plan Mr. Clarke and I had discussed.

Jason Field smiled. "It's liable to work. For that price you might get the Harris family to sell out too. They're in the same boat as the Dawsons."

"I'd been thinking about that," I said. Out of the corner

of my eye I saw Mr. Clarke's head raise up. Directing myself to Mr. Field I asked, "Would you offer to buy out the Harrises on a note if I bought the place from you just as I have agreed to do with Mr. Clarke?"

"Well, boy, it's one thing to sign a note. The time comes when an obligation has to be met. We could be in for years of drought. Have you thought of that? Just remember this, always remember it, that which is borrowed must be paid back."

"I sure have thought of it. What we haven't talked about is their herds. Without ranches they'll have to sell them too. I'll grant you they are skin and bones now, but it's my thought, if the rains don't come, to move them north. We might even have to go as far as Oklahoma, but I hear they've had rain there and plenty of it. If we can lease pasture land and fatten up the cattle, because of the low cost we'll have in them, we should be able to make our note and interest payments and keep things going for quite a spell."

"Maybe so, maybe so." Mr. Field and Mr. Clarke fretted and there was a considerable amount of conversation. But the prospect of range war overshadowed everything. All things considered, the suggestions I had made seemed to them to be the lesser of two evils. "I can't say I much care for this plan," Mr. Field said, but then he agreed. He and Ben Jordan got ready to set off toward the Harris ranch. Mr. Field was never one to put things off. The marshal stood by his horse, tightening the cinch, and he said he was going to put all parties on notice that if there was any more gunplay they would have to reckon with him personally. He said, "If it gets where I can't handle it we'll send for the Texas Rangers, and then there will be pure hell to pay." He turned to me. "This warning includes you, Tom. I've heard about what happened at Three Points. Two men are dead, one of them by your hand. They admit that the man you shot went for his gun first, but I'll have no more of this, do you hear?" Then he said, "You have killed sixteen men, not counting probably causing John Dawson's death. There is always a bad end waiting for a gunfighter. I keep telling you this but you don't act like you want to listen. I had hoped you were finally ready to settle down."

I didn't have an answer for him, and he looked at me a long spell before he rode off.

I spent the rest of the morning with Sally and Rebecca and the Clarkes. Culley had been out with the cattle the last few times I had been over, and it was good to see him. I told him all the details about the showdown at Three Points and about my brush with Earl and Billy Dawson.

Culley began to joke. It was his way. "They are going to be mighty careful about sending men into the Lazy E at night in the future. They will be in mortal fear that it might earn a return visit by the Rattlesnake Kid."

"The who?"

"Ain't you heard? There is a dime novel that was published back East about you. It's called *The Rattlesnake Kid.* It stretches the truth here and there, even though it is supposed to be based on your life. I've got a copy right here."

I looked at the blue paperback book. It had a drawing of a cross between Buffalo Bill and a sheep on the cover, it seemed to me, for the person shown there had curly sheepskin leggins with the wool on, like I hear they have in Montana, up in cold country. I never had a pair of chaps like that in my life. The character had blazing eyes and two six-shooters, one in each hand. The title was *Tom English, the Rattlesnake Kid,* and it was written in smaller type, "Killer of 15 men when only 19 years of age." In larger type it said, "The True Story of the Meanest Man in West Texas."

I felt absolutely sickened, but Culley was doubled up he was laughing so hard.

That afternoon I rode home. Mr. Field and Ben Jordan had told me that they would pass by that way after seeing the folks at the Harris ranch. They had agreed to stay the night after I pressed the point. Company would be welcome, for the place was lonely as all get-out without Sally and Rebecca.

It was after dark when they got there. They came down the slope from the house to the river, where Benito and the cowboys not on guard duty were fixing a big spread. They had a large fire going and around it on several upright stakes they were roasting young kid goats. Our vaqueros were as glad as I was to have some company. It was a change from looking over our shoulders all the time, looking for the glint of a rifle.

Later we hunkered down over plates of the cabrito and frijoles which had been made pepper hot with chili tepins and jalapeños. We had coffee and tequila and most of us got about half drunk, even Mr. Field, to my considerable surprise.

He said, "Tom, in spite of the trouble you have been in, and the worry you have caused me, you are as close to a son as I've got. You have stood up on your back legs and made a place for yourself." Maybe it was the liquor talking, but it pleased me a great deal to hear what he said.

He was proud of the negotiation job he had done with the Harris family. They had made a deal and had shook hands on it. In this country that means more than a notarized contract, signed and sealed, would have in most other places. It was all to be finalized the next week at Jedediah

Jackson's office in Santa Rita. He was everybody's land lawyer for he was the only lawyer in town.

Ben Jordan said, "If these business arrangements go through and the Dawsons and Harrises move on I still won't rest easy until their hired guns leave. They have come in here spoiling for a fight, and all of a sudden it looks like they could find themselves out of a job, with Tom English, the man they have planned to face, sitting pretty."

I didn't really have an answer for him but I said, "The first thing is to get their bosses out, and then you should be able to chouse them around and move them on."

"I hope so. I don't know if it will be all that easy." His face had a somber look to it.

The next morning they rode off in separate ways. Ben Jordan gave a strong warning to me and to Benito and left for the Dawson ranch, where he planned to say the same thing to Billy and Earl Dawson. He maintained that he had already laid down the law to Pete Harris, who was the head of that family, and who was one tough hombre from what everybody said.

Things were quiet for the next week. The reports I got from Mr. Sam Clarke were encouraging. He had completed the deal with the Dawsons and now had legal title to their land. They had driven a hard bargain, though, and he'd had to pay extra for the houses, barns, and improvements. He had also bought their herd for cash, but he said it was at about ten cents on the dollar as to their worth.

Then Culley brought Sally and Rebecca back home, together with the good news that Mr. Field had bought out the Harris family. They must have been talking to the Dawsons, for they insisted on the same deal for their improvements and also demanded a cash sale for their herd. The rest was a surprise. Sally's older sister, Agnes, was going to marry J. D. Turner, who ranched west of Ozona.

The Turners were said to own a large amount of Crockett County, and that county is mighty big.

As we sat there talking Culley said, "Have you been noticing the sky out west?"

I confessed that as good as his news was I had been listening with only half an ear. I had been paying too much attention to the heavy black clouds that were building up. The thunderheads loomed high above us and chain lightning would bolt down every few minutes, and the wind had picked up until now it was swirling and gusting. All of a sudden a dust-and-sand storm so thick that you actually couldn't see twenty feet in front of you was upon us.

Culley leaned into it and led his horse toward the barn. He unsaddled him and turned him out in the corral and came lumbering back, head down, into the house just as a bolt of lightning hit the big pecan tree next to the little cooling shed we had for milk right behind the house. It sounded like the whole world had blown up. At the same time the first real rain in over two years began. It started slow—just a big drop here and then one there. Suddenly it slashed down almost horizontally, the wind was blowing that hard.

We had been running all over the house pulling down windows to keep the thick dust out, and we all came back together on the screened-in front porch. I guess I never heard such a wonderful noise or saw such a marvelous sight. And the smell of that rain goes beyond description. The dust was completely gone now, and the wind was not as high. The rain began to fall in earnest in a real gully washer. Rebecca crawled up in my lap, her face frightened. Then I realized that she couldn't remember what rain looked like.

It kept going for one hour and then for another. Though it was only midday it was almost as dark as night. Then I thought of the cattle. Our entire herd was down by the few remaining holes of water, up and down the Concho. I had never seen it rain anywhere near as hard as this, but even with fairly good rains I knew what could happen. It would almost invariably cause a quick rise. This time there was no doubt about what was going to happen. We had to get set for a real flood. It could be a disaster. The herd that we had worked with for nearly four years could be wiped out in a matter of hours.

I told Culley about my fear and it didn't take him a minute to realize what was bothering me. While he explained to Sally I ran to put on my hat and yellow slicker and spurs. Then we went to the bunkhouse and told Benito and the men what had to be done. We had to get our cattle to high ground in a hurry. We could only hope that the other ranchers downstream would be doing the same thing with their herds.

We ran out, sliding and splashing, and first one damn thing and then another would happen. We all felt like a bunch of schoolkids playing outside in the rain. What I'm trying to say is how exciting it was, how much fun it was, even sopping wet the way we were.

It was a mud-and-rain carnival, roping our horses in the corral, and trying to saddle them with the thunder and lightning going on. The horses were naturally as spooked by all of our running around in our yellow slickers as they were by the crazy weather, and even well-broke horses were acting like colts. Several men got thrown, and more than one horse fell trying to unload his rider, bucking and rearing on the slippery, muddy ground. But then we were mounted and hightailing it for the Concho. I saw one of our boys going like a bat out of the bad place when a bolt of lightning hit him and his horse, and they went down in a wild tumble. Neither one of them moved. They were smoking.

That is a terrible, literal fact. Smoke was coming from them and the horse was black and split open where the lightning bolt had hit him. I never saw anything like it in my born days. Horses attract lightning. Everyone knows that. But knowing it and seeing it are two different things. We had a cowboy take the dead man back to the ranch, and the rest of us, saying our prayers that the lightning wouldn't hit us, rode on at a dead run through the driving rain toward the river. The fun had gone out of the day, but the urgency sure as hell hadn't.

When we got to the river Culley and Benito took half the men and went to the other side, where hundreds of thin cattle stood by the river the way they do, facing into the wind and rain. I have never understood why they do that. Horses will stand with their backs to the wind every time.

I watched the seven men waving their hats and ropes and hollering like banshees. The cattle got to moving and then lumbered into a slow rocking run. Then they started toward high ground on the other side of the river, and the five men on my side followed me as we headed south. The rain never let up an instant through all of this time. We kept finding pockets of cattle here and there and we would drive them up from the low ground along the river. In a few hours it looked like most of the work had been done and I waved my arm at Benito, across the way, to come back while he still could.

He and Culley and the cowboys with them came single file along a steep trail that led sharply down the river bank to the gravel bottom of the Concho. The river itself at the time wasn't six inches deep except for about four feet at the edge, where it was more standing in pools than running. There it might have been a few feet deep. Just as Benito started up the bank on our side we heard it. It was roaring with a noise like a dozen trains might make. All of us saw it at the same time. A wall of water at least twelve feet high hurtled toward the helpless men and horses down in between the two steep banks. I had my rope in my hand and hollered just as I threw it to Culley. He and Benito were in the lead and both of them made a lunge for the rope. Culley caught it, but Benito missed. The next thing I knew was that the wall of water hit with brutal, wrenching force. I had the rope hitched around my saddle horn, and Bess slipped on the mud when Culley hit the end of the line with a jerk. She got her balance and we started backward, but it was way too easy. I had one hand on the rope and I pulled on it and knew that Culley had been torn loose.

It was muddy and slick and the rain came down so hard I could hardly see a thing. The water looked black, and trees and horses and once in a while a man would appear and then disappear back in the torn froth of the raging currents. I was on a high bank and Bess was galloping alongside the river. The bank on the other side opened up and the water spread far out. In just a little while the Concho, that had narrowed down to around four feet, was almost a hundred yards wide. It must have been raining just as hard upriver to the north of us.

Bess was stretched out in a run and I hardly felt the limbs that slapped and scratched my face. I could taste blood as I kept following the wildly rushing river. Then I heard a cry and pulled Bess back on her haunches. It took me a second but then I saw Benito and he was holding onto the bent branches of a willow tree with one hand, and he had his other arm around Culley. I was afraid to throw him the rope. He couldn't turn loose to catch it without dropping Culley. He was too far out in the river for me to get to him. I tied the end of my rope to the saddle horn and got off Bess. Standing as close to the edge as I dared, I built a loop and threw it wide open and hard and clean down over Benito's shoulders. He let go of the tree and grabbed hold of the rope with his right hand while I began pulling him toward the river bank. He held onto Culley with his left arm for dear life. I could make out the strain on his face, and I knew a flash of terror, for Culley's eyes were closed and his mouth was open.

I backed Bess and pulled the two muddy, battered men up on the bank. A tree or something must have hit Culley, for he was out cold and there was a cut on his forehead that was bleeding, but his heartbeat was strong and his breathing seemed normal. How Benito ever caught hold of him God only knows. We stretched him out on the bank and he began to come around. About this time the other five men who had been with me rode up. They had managed to help three more of our boys out of the flash flood, but it looked like two were lost.

When Culley came to his senses they put him behind me on Bess, and the men who had been with me carried Benito and the three wet and beaten cowboys. The horses, which had been so frisky that morning, were now so whipped down that none of them raised sand about carrying double. Two of the men who had been fished out of the flood appeared to have broken arms and maybe broken ribs, and all were terribly bruised. They were still too stunned to show how afraid they had been.

The picture of that solid wall of black water, with foam and curls of waves at the top, is frozen in my mind. I'll never forget the sight of it.

It took us until dark to get home and by then the rain was settling down to a slow, steady downpour. Sally was frantic when we got there. She had expected us hours before. It is human nature when you have been scared about kinfolks who turn out to be all right to get mad, and Sally showed just how human she was. She got mad as a wet hen and for the first time since I had known her I heard her utter a curse word. She said, "Damn you, Tom English, where have you been?" Then she saw Culley and Benito and the hurt cowboys and she said, "Oh, my God!"

CHAPTER 15

It turned out that Culley wasn't as bad off as he looked, and inside of a few days he had left for the Clarke ranch, raising hell and laughing all at the same time, according to his way. Before he left he made Benito accept his silver-buckled belt as a present. He just wouldn't accept no for an answer. I had told Culley about Benito holding on to him for dear life with one arm and hanging on to the willow with his free hand, with the floodwaters of the Concho tearing at him. It made a deep impression on Culley. "If he had lost his grip we both could have drowned. The average man would have let me go and saved his own skin. He put his life on the line for mine." So, like I said, with fussing and laughing, he left—but I saw a serious side to Culley at that time. And Benito had made a permanent close friend and he knew it.

The ranchers downriver had suffered the loss of a great many cattle, far more than we had. They hadn't thought to try to save them. But they had not lost any men and, of course, we had. It struck me that there can be times when lack of action is a lot sounder than action, though that goes against the things all kids in this country are taught.

Mr. Field had closed the deal with Pete Harris at Jedediah Jackson's office before the rains had come. His foreman had been present at their roundup and had a tally on the horses and cattle, and these were purchased for cash. As I've said, they almost gave the stock away, but they stuck by their bargain and had seemed relieved about getting out. They apparently had been afraid that the drought and lack of access to the Concho would break them. Yet now the rains had come, just a short time after the Harris and Dawson families had sold out. I could imagine the rage and frustration they must feel. On the other hand, there would be droughts in the future. I honestly believed that they would be better off to move on and get established somewhere else. At least that is what I kept telling myself.

I went to Jedediah Jackson's office and Mr. Jason Field and Mr. Sam Clarke sold me the Harris and Dawson ranches for what they had paid for them. Then we went to the bank and I borrowed enough to pay for the cattle and horses on both ranches. I was considerably pleased to find I was able to borrow without anyone going on my note. Max Hall, the president of the First National Bank, said, "You have taken care of your obligations in the past right well, and I expect you will keep on honoring those that you make. For another thing, you've bought this stock at one hell of a price, and now that you have had rain you should be in shape to make a killing." He harrumphed and looked embarrassed. He said, "By that I mean to say that you should make a handsome profit."

When we finished at the bank we rode out to the Lower Ranch and had a big lunch that Mr. Field's bunkhouse cook had fixed. It wasn't fancy, but it was filling. Later we sat on the veranda and Jason Field said to Mr. Clarke, "Sam, I remember hiring this youngster when he was seventeen years old. He wasn't dry behind the ears and, except for some natural ability with horses, you wouldn't have picked him out of a crowd as having any special capabilities. As a matter of fact he was shy and seemed a little confused to me most of the time." He was having a good time right then making me feel embarrassed.

Mr. Field went on, "I'll not forget the night he came in after he had shot Jack Malone. It was self-defense, I'm sure of that, although to this day I have never figured out how he did it. Did you know he was packing a single-action .44 that he had to cock? Well, we don't want to dwell on those things. What I was talking about was how unlikely it seemed to me when he first hired on as a horse wrangler to think how he would turn out. I don't mean the gunplay. Those things have a way of happening, especially with men who won't back down. That's another thing—Tom as a kid looked so damn young—he looked younger than his age, you would never have figured him to be one who could not be shoved."

He took off his hat and passed his hand through his hair, and then put his hat back on. "I had some rough experiences growing up. This is a hard country and some terrible things can happen. It is just the way it is. But after all is said and done, here sits Tom, alive and well, a friend now—and like the son I never had—and he is your son-in-law. He has got the world by the tail with a downhill pull, I'd say. God almighty! Think of it. Tom owns the Lazy E, that's ten sections, and he has just bought the Harris ranch, which has seventy-five sections, and the Dawson ranch, which has ninety sections." He took the stub of a yellow pencil out of his shirt pocket and did some hurried calculations. Then he said, "By all that's holy, that comes to a hundred and seventy-five sections altogether." Then he said, I suppose to put me in my place, "Let's see, I should have around about"—as if he didn't know exactly; he made a few more scribbles—"just at two hundred and six sections along the Concho in the Upper and Lower ranches."

Mr. Clarke pulled a sack of Bull Durham out of his

pocket and rolled a cigarette. When he had leaned into his cupped hands and lit it, he took a deep breath and reared back in his chair. When he talked after that little wisps of smoke kept coming out of his mouth. "Well, Jason, he's got some work to do to pay off his notes." He looked at me with a twinkle in his eyes. "It will probably take you all your life, but you're going to make my granddaughter a mighty wealthy little girl."

Then Jason Field said, "I had a talk with the U.S. marshal while Tom was in the bank. It looks like he has been able to run all of those hired guns out of this part of the country. Pete Harris and Billy Dawson had hired a passel of them, but thanks be to God, that particular trouble has passed."

I took my leave then, with thanks to them for helping me, and met Benito at Three Points, where he was waiting for me. We rode over to the Dawson ranch and hired their foreman on the spot. His name was Ted Carrothers and I had met him a few times before. He was an old-timer and was responsible. To the best of my knowledge he had never taken part in any of the gunplay against our people at the Lazy E. I told Ted to hire the hands he needed and to bring the stock in to the Concho whenever they needed to, as the river was still up over its banks and there sure wasn't much question of a water shortage. I told him where I wanted gates put in the fence and left that chore up to him.

The next day I did the same thing with Osie Black, the longtime foreman at the Harris ranch. He was another old hand who knew his land and stock well. I gave him a free hand to hire the cowboys he would need as well.

When I finally got back to the Lazy E I was tired but happy, and more than a little excited.

I sat with Sally and Rebecca on the porch after supper

and watched the fireflies and told stories to Rebecca. Then, after she went to bed, Sally said, "Tom, you promised me once before to put up your gun. I can understand why you had to use it again. It just couldn't be helped, it looked like. But I'm going to hold you to your word." She looked at me long and hard. I suppose I must have had a stubborn expression on my face, for she began to cry and she said, "Please, Tom."

Well, hell, what could I do? There wasn't no choice at all. I had to agree. That night I cleaned the Colt .45 that Jason Field had given me. After oiling it carefully to guard against rust, I tried its heft and marveled again at its balance. It just felt *right*, somehow, in my hand. Then I saddle-soaped the cartridge belt and scabbard, and after holstering the six-gun, I wrapped it up very carefully in oilskin and put it in a drawer of the dresser in our bedroom, underneath some dress shirts Sally had bought me that I never had worn and likely never would.

I can remember so clearly the moment I closed the drawer. I seemed to hear a voice and it asked, "When will you wear this gun again?"

CHAPTER 16

With the help of Mr. Jason Field and Mr. Sam Clarke in a year my three ranches were pretty well organized. I ended up with a good manager and a foreman under him for each of them. Benito Acosta ran the Lazy E, Ted Carrothers was on top of things at the old Dawson ranch, and Osie Black was in charge at the Harris place. Each one of them had chosen a good man to handle the cowboys. I spent my time planning as well as working on the finances, although few days passed that I didn't ride out to check over the stock. I couldn't help but pitch in when there were new horses to break. I would take a few falls, or get banged against a snubbing post or a fence, but that goes along with cowboyin'. I enjoyed being out of doors. That is what I loved, but more and more of my time was being spent at a desk. It like to have drove me crazy. Another thing was the damned traveling. It seemed that I was meeting myself coming and going as I went to and from Fort Worth. That was, and still is, the best place in Texas to buy and sell cattle. Mr. Field was bound and determined to see me go all the way with Herefords, so we had one hell of a roundup on the Harris and Dawson ranches; everyone still used the old names and I guess they always will no matter how long they're in my family. Then we got the stock to Fort Worth. Prices had boomed in the last six months and there was a fine market for beef. So we sold out every last longhorn we had, and made what seemed to me like an unconscionable profit.

After getting the cattle at the end of the drought at around ten cents on the dollar, I had gotten them good and fat, for with the rains came grass and weeds. The land was newborn. We didn't sell the stock until they had spent a month in the feedlots in Fort Worth and, as luck would have it, the delay of that month was when the price of beef went up so much. Well, better lucky than smart, like they say.

I can't explain why, but a sadness came over me as the last of the longhorns were driven off. I guess I should have kept a few of them. Too many things were changing and I wasn't sure I liked all of it. I had been free as the wind, and now I was tied down as any clerk on earth. "Hellfire and damnation!" I hollered. Benito was with me and he looked at me like I had gone plumb off my head.

I had more than enough money to buy my breeding stock. I got most of the Hereford cows in the Texas Panhandle at the Anderson and Johnson ranches at high but fair prices. Mr. Field had bought four fine herd bulls in Kansas City. They were the early strain of what came to be the Prince Domino line of Hereford bulls, which won more than their share of grand championship ribbons at the fat stock shows in later years. Mr. Field kept bending over backward to help me, and nothing would do but he must give me the two best bulls he had.

Culley Clarke was with me when this happened. Whenever I had good fortune Culley would be as happy as I was. It worked both ways, of course. I had gotten even closer to Culley through the years. It was a lot more than his being my brother-in-law. He was the only close friend I ever had. I don't mean to say I wasn't close to Mr. Field and Mr. Clarke, but they were more like parents, in a way. I would help out at the Clarke ranch and Culley would come over and help out at our place. There was nothing I might ask that he would hesitate about, and that part of it held true when he would ask me for help. I would have gone to hell and back for him. We never talked about this kind of thing, but we both knew how things stood.

Well, anyway, Culley got just as excited as I did about those bulls. A herd bull is something to see, with broad, thick horns curving down, and huge shoulders. In them was the appearance and reality of raw power, like they could walk right through a barn if they had a mind to. My first concern was to keep them separated so they wouldn't kill each other. As a kid I had once seen two bulls work up to a fight. They stood facing each other, about thirty feet apart, and threw great clouds of dirt and dust over their backs, pawing at the ground and bellowing. And then, with the preliminaries over, they had gone full tilt into each other. I'll never forget the incredible sight, or the sound of crashing bone and horn smashing together. I'm sure it could have been heard for over a mile. I got to thinking about this problem and then I thought about the system Mr. Field had of rotating his herd between the Upper and Lower ranches. I rode out to Three Points one day and was sitting there in the shade, the way you do when you're waiting around, with my right leg hooked over the saddle horn. I was chewing the sweetness out of a hard yellow mesquite bean, with my hat shoved back on my head, when it came to me what should be done. It seemed so simple that I don't know why we hadn't thought about it before.

What had to be done, of course, was to cross-fence the ranches. We had dug big dirt tanks to catch the rain runoff, so the location of these more or less controlled how we would lay out our pastures. We bought the bob wire and supplies and Benito got a big crew together. The fence layers were mainly from Mexico, and some might later on work out as cowboys. We had a large number of Mexican cowboys and they were the salt of the earth. At the Lazy E ranches (we used that brand all over now) they knew they would get fair treatment. This was sure as hell not the case elsewhere. Especially in the towns, where the poor wetbacks were treated worse than dogs. But with us we measured a man by how he could handle his job.

During the time the fences were being built we had an unbelievably good calf crop. The regular rains, that I knew we couldn't count on, continued. It was like I was being helped out of debt. Though I had figured on being in the hole for many years to come, the last cent I owed the bank and some that I owed Mr. Clarke and Mr. Field was paid by the time we got our last fence in place. The Dawsons and Harrises had been paid off by Mr. Field and Mr. Clarke, and I heard that they had found smaller ranches out farther west.

It took the better part of two years to get the Harris and Dawson ranches I had bought fenced, and then all three ranches cross-fenced. Culley had followed suit and was fencing the Clarke ranch, and it wasn't long before Mr. Field, after raising all kinds of hell about it, did the same. He realized he could move his cattle from one pasture to another a lot easier than he could move them twenty miles through the Clarke spread from the Upper Ranch to the Lower Ranch and back again. And now that the Clarke ranch was being fenced it would be damn near impossible to take a big herd through.

It was easier to find the stock and to keep a good count on them with just a certain number in each pasture. It kept the land from being overgrazed in one area and undergrazed in another. Like I was saying, I can't imagine why we hadn't done it before.

During all of this time only a few bad things happened. That's how most of us mark the way time passes—like the year the barn burned or something along those lines. The first thing was when Sally and Culley's sister, Agnes, who had married a Turner from Crockett County, died in childbirth. The baby died too. We rode out to Ozona for the funeral, about ninety-five miles from Santa Rita. By the time we got there Agnes had already been buried, but the preacher held another service for us. I couldn't help but worry about Sally for she cried like her heart would break. Her father and mother sat with Culley and Sally and me. I noticed how old they looked all of a sudden.

Agnes had been built like Sally, narrow through the hips, and I recalled the ordeal Sally had been through when Rebecca had come. A shock ran through me when I realized I might have lost them just as now we had lost Agnes and her baby.

After the memorial service Culley and I rode out to the Sanders ranch, for they were known to have good horses. They had a fine roan stallion that we bought as a present for Mr. Sam Clarke. While we were there my eye was taken by some thoroughbreds they had bought in Kentucky the year before. They wouldn't sell any but they were sending a buyer back to Kentucky the next month and I put up the money for ten mares. I could just imagine the foals we would get crossing this racehorse stock with old Dan. He was known in our part of the country as the best stud around.

Mr. Clarke had tears in his eyes when we gave him the roan. He simply couldn't talk. Mrs. Clarke came up and hugged me long and hard. I had never really felt that I knew Mrs. Clarke as I did her husband, in spite of the fact that she had nursed me when I had been shot up, and through the years had been as sweet as could be. But I got well acquainted with her on that trip. She told me many stories on the road back about life in the early days, and about what Sally had been like as a little girl. It seems that a time comes in a person's life when it is important to talk about the past, about how things used to be.

When we got to Santa Rita, Culley and I stayed behind to see about how the markets were going for beef. Sally went to the Clarke ranch with her parents to wait for us.

By then Santa Rita had a telegraph operator and we found out as much as we could about beef prices there in the telegraph office. After that we went down to the Main Street Bar. I recalled having once been requested to drink elsewhere, but I didn't like to go into the bar that had formerly been known as Malone's Saloon, though it had a different name now. The only other place, the Buckhorn, didn't appeal to me. It was small and crowded.

We had no more than sat down at a table and ordered our drinks when Billy Dawson and old man Pete Harris came up. Billy had been drinking. He said, in a thick-tongued way, "What is a farmer doing in here?"

You need to understand the contempt that cowboys all felt about farmers to appreciate what he was saying. The reason he brought this up, I suppose, had to do with the fact that I had put two hundred acres in hay on each of my three ranches. I needed hay for the horses and for the bulls and show stock we were pampering, and it seemed foolish to buy it.

I didn't answer him and he turned ugly. Naturally, everyone knew I didn't carry a gun anymore. In addition, he had drunk a good amount of Dutch courage.

Billy said, "You've got rich from the cattle you stole off of us. You fenced the river and stole our ranches too. We would *never* have sold out to you, and we told you so. God damn you, Tom English! You cheated and tricked us!" His voice was wild and loud and hard to understand. He hollered, "*Our* cattle, *our* land, that is what has made you rich, you son of a bitch."

I could feel my face get red and hot and Culley put his hand on my arm to calm me down.

I could hear my voice say, in a hard way, "You know I'm not wearing a gun. But I can borrow Culley's and we can go outside in the street if that's what you have in mind."

Billy's face broke up and he actually looked like he might cry, though he didn't. That definitely was not what he had in mind. He started to the door of the saloon with Pete Harris. When he got there he turned around and said, "You killed my daddy, too."

Then he went out but Harris stood there just a minute. He said, "English, someday a man in black is going to ride into this town and send for you. And you'll come. When you do, you'll die." He turned and walked out the door.

I had another whiskey and took my time drinking it. I have had my share of threats. Yet somehow this one bothered me more than the others.

CHAPTER 17

Culley had been playing poker at the stockyards in Fort Worth, and when he got to the hotel I could tell he had won, for he had that funny grin on his face. I never knew a grown man who was more of a child at heart. He had a bottle of good bourbon in his suitcase and wanted to celebrate, so we sat in my hotel room and had a few drinks.

"Look here at all this money," Culley said. He pulled rolls of it out from all of his pockets and piled it on the table. "Hell, I don't even know how much there is."

I felt content. I wasn't all excited like he was, but I had a warm, relaxed feeling. I was wearing a new pair of custom-made boots that I'd been fitted for the last time I had been in Fort Worth. I always wear regular work clothes, but by that time I must have had fifteen or twenty different pairs of boots. It was a tom fool thing to do, but I enjoyed it. And these new ones were soft and felt good.

I put the new boots up on the coffee table in front of the couch and leaned back. "Culley," I said, "I ran across something today that could change things for us. There was a big display of windmills over at the auction barn, and I visited with the folks there who were selling them. I have bought the parts for five and I hired their salesman to come help us put them up. He is coming with a drilling rig. If there's no water then I'm out some money. But if there is, it could end up with our having regular water in every pasture. We've been lucky ever since the big flood, but we know the Concho can get mighty low—too low to take care of our herds."

Culley argued that I should have bought one windmill and tried it out, but I explained that the big cost was getting the drilling rig and the man with the know-how. If we did hit water, why we'd sink four more holes and have five wells.

Culley shook his head and told me I was ruining the West, and where would it all end, and so forth, and then he got all duded up to find a lady friend for the evening.

Left to myself I drew out a rough map of the ranches and decided where I'd like wells if I could get the water. The man I'd hired had said he was real good at "witching" wells, that he took a Y cut from a willow branch with a fork in it, and he could tell where the water was when the long end of the stick, which he would hold just so, pointed down. I didn't have much faith in that, but he acted like he knew what he was talking about.

It took two days for Culley to get caught up on fancy ladies and whiskey and card playing. By the end of that time he could hardly stand up, and we started on the long road back, at least two hundred miles, to our homes. There was talk of the Santa Fe railroad putting in a spur clear to Santa Rita someday but that sounded like wishful thinking.

When the first well came in, right at the house on the Lazy E, I got more excited than Culley had when he had won all that money at his card game. I contracted then and there for the wagons and for the supplies to bring out fifteen more windmills. Then we went to work in earnest. As each well was completed we built a big storage tank and also a long trough for the stock. The fellow we had hired in Fort Worth proved to be well worth his salt. While it is true that we hit a few dry holes, we hit more with water.

We fixed float valves in the water troughs so that the well

water in the storage tanks would flow down by gravity to refill them when the floats went down so far. It was just like a miracle. We had been walking the weight off our stock driving them to the river, or to the pastures with water in dirt tank reservoirs. The less we had to do of this the better off the stock would be. And even more important, when the drought came, we would have water for the cattle and horses.

With this in mind we doubled the acreage we had in hay and began accumulating large stacks of it. When the drought came, and come it would, we would be able to keep most of our stock, if not fat, at least alive. In good times it was essential to worry about the bad times.

I had talked over these theories with Culley and his dad and with Mr. Field, and they were interested, but skeptical. But in my view it was the rancher's salvation. It was my opinion that with fencing and cross-fencing to protect the pastures from overgrazing, and with windmills to provide regular water, we could stand any reasonable drought.

It was along about this time that I began to cull out my herd and thin it down. If anything, I was determined to undergraze my pastures. The practice was to put all the stock on them that they could stand, but this meant that when the drought hit, the pastures were so thin they turned to dust in no time at all. I was determined to keep this from happening on my property.

It took over a year to get more dirt tanks dug, and to get our windmills in operation. I had stayed so busy that the time had just slipped by. One evening I rode to the house and took a long hot bath. I was bone-tired. Sally was fixing a big meal. She said she was going to put some meat on my bones. I had just dressed and put on a pair of soft leather boots that were as comfortable as house shoes when I heard someone riding up.

I went outside as Culley came up, his horse white with lather and breathing hard. Culley got down and came up to me. "Tom, Jason Field is bad hurt. His horse stepped in a prairie dog hole while he was trying to rope a dogie, and he went down hard. It broke the horse's leg and they had to shoot him. Jason's men were afraid to take him to Santa Rita, so they rode for the doc. One of the Field cowboys came to our place. He said that Jason is asking for you."

Sally had come out and heard, so she said to me, "You sit down and eat a bit, Tom, before you go." But of course I couldn't do that. I put on my spurs and my hat and sent for a fast young horse we called Joe, for no good reason except that with more than a hundred horses you run out of names.

Joe was a three-year-old by Dan out of Bess. This young horse meant a hell of a lot to me. Bess had been the best mount I'd ever had. In my view she had the best conformation of any quarterhorse I had ever seen. At her distance it would be hard to find a horse to keep up with her, although over the long pull Dan could have outlasted her when he was at his prime. I had high hopes for their colt, and he was proving to be quick. With time I expected he would build up his endurance.

While one of the boys saddled Joe for me I laid out a loop and caught a fresh mount for Culley. Then the two of us left. From the Lazy E headquarters to Mr. Field's ranch house at the Lower Ranch was a good thirty miles. As we rode I thought of the things Mr. Field had done for me. (Culley and most others called him "Jason," but I couldn't; I'd been brought up to call older folk "Mr.") Well, he had sure done a lot. I would probably not be alive but for him. I owed my life in all likelihood to the old gunfighter, for without the skills he had taught me, and the practice he had demanded, I would have died at eighteen in Villa Plata.

When we got to the Lower Ranch it was past midnight. Doc Starret's buggy was hitched out front alongside of several horses with the Clarke big C brand on their hips. Mr. Sam would be inside, I was sure of that.

I was surprised to find that Jedediah Jackson was in the house talking to Mr. Clarke when I got there. I had never seen the old lawyer when he wasn't completely composed, but now his face was drawn and his eyes had tears in them. The three of us walked into the bedroom and I was shocked at Mr. Field's face, for it was gray with pain. He took my hand when I was next to him and tried to smile. He said in a voice so soft I had to lean down to hear him, "You've meant a lot to me." Then, at that minute, a long sigh came from him and his hand loosened in mine. Doc Starret was by the bed in an instant with his stethoscope and he said, "He's dead."

It just knocked me down, in a way of speaking. It hit me so much harder than I would ever have thought it would.

We held the funeral where I knew he would have liked it, up on a hill that overlooked the Lower Ranch headquarters. People had come from many a mile around, and just as the funeral was over the damnedest thing happened: about twenty or thirty of Mr. Field's horses came galloping up to within a hundred yards of us. They stood there just that instant, outlined against the sunset behind them, looking at us with their heads up and their ears cocked forward. Horses are always so blamed curious. They do things like that. But it was like they were saying goodbye. I don't expect there was a dry eye among the people there.

We went back to the house where the women had brought a spread of fried chicken and biscuits and the like. Later the menfolk sat together in the drawing room and told stories about Mr. Field, most of them funny. It seems like after a funeral people want to look back on the good times.

The next morning I went to see Jedediah Jackson at his law office. He had asked me to drop by when we had sat together after the funeral. When I went in he turned around in his bentwood swivel chair. I sat down while he filled his pipe and lit it. Jedediah spoke seldom and always thought awhile beforehand.

He sat there working on his pipe and I looked at the lawbooks in shelves from floor to ceiling and at his big oak desk. The desk faced a wall and had a hutch on it with doors. He reached up and opened one of the doors and I saw dozens of little wooden cubbyholes filled with blue-backed legal documents. He pulled out one of these, closed the door, and turned around again to face me.

"Tom, I am reasonably sure you don't know why I asked for you to be here today."

I took off my hat. "No, sir, I reckon I don't."

He smiled a little. "Jason Field was one of the closest friends I have ever had. I don't know if you were aware of it, there is no real reason why you should, but I came here from East Texas because of my friendship for him. I would still be living in Nacogdoches if he and I hadn't gotten acquainted. I have never known a finer man. We met when he was just a young man, only nineteen. I was almost exactly seven years older; both of us were born in March. I was practicing law when we got acquainted. He had been in a shooting scrape, he was pushed into it, but the folks in the little town where this happened were after his hide. Well, to make a long story short, I got him off scot-free. He stayed in trouble on and off for some years after that, but he finally settled here with an inheritance from his grandfather; and he started all over. That's when he wrote to me that it was a good place to live—that a man could try for a fresh start. For some reason that idea made a tremendous impact on me. I had been going nowhere in particular and I was more than a little depressed. So I up and moved out to West Texas, and I've been here ever since."

He smiled at me. Then he said, "Tom, you would be surprised at how often Jason talked to me about you. Few weeks went by that we didn't get together. He said he saw himself in you. He saw in you the son he never had." Mr. Jackson puffed on his pipe and I looked at him through the smoke. Then he said, "That's why he made you his sole heir and beneficiary."

The words didn't come through to me. I heard them but I couldn't quite understand what they meant. Mr. Jackson said, "Here, I'm going to pour you a drink." He smiled in a sad way. "Jason had a good life and his great pleasure in the last few years was thinking about doing this for you and your family." He paused and then he said, "I am in no way soliciting business, but I want you to consult with me as a friend and with Max Hall over at the First National Bank too. He has good judgment and you can depend on his advice."

He stopped talking for a minute, and then he said, "Are you all right, Tom? You're pale as a ghost."

I did what Mr. Jackson and Max Hall advised me to do. It proved to be good counsel. Mr. Jackson got the will probated and all the property put in my name. With the money in the bank that Mr. Field had saved I had a very sizable stake. As a matter of fact, I was astonished at how much it was. I visited with Mr. Hall and paid off my bank loans for the windmills and the stock of cattle I had been buying. I paid off my debts to Mr. Sam Clarke, and I bought mindmills and supplies to get good water for all the pastures on the Lower and Upper ranches. My work was cut out for me, for they totaled 206 sections. The Lazy E and the Harris and Dawson ranches, which I had now finished paying for, came to 175 sections. (My remaining debt to Mr. Jason Field was canceled, of course, since it was one of his assets, and everything he had owned was left to me.) When the properties were added together I now owned 381 sections in all. Outside of the King Ranch in South Texas and the XIT in the Texas Panhandle, I wasn't aware of many men with more land, although perhaps there were some.

I suppose everyone who gets money all of a sudden acts like a fool. I tried not to, but there was one thing I did do. I got started on one hell of a big house on the Upper Ranch. It took a year to build, but even if it was extravagant, I would do the same thing all over again.

Mrs. Clarke, Sally and Culley's mother, had died a few weeks after Mr. Field from what Doc Starret said was a weak heart. She had been sick on and off for some time but no one had put much stock in her complaints. Now we all felt guilty. Sally wanted to be closer to her dad, which was understandable. It wasn't an easy ride from the Lazy E. We decided to build on the Upper Ranch, between the Clarke and Lazy E ranches, and within a day's easy ride to the Lower Ranch, where I would have to be spending some time from now on, so it made sense. When you decide you want to do something you can always talk yourself into it.

The house we built had two stories and a wide veranda all around it. We had big stone fireplaces in almost every room, and a fenced yard for flowers and as a place for Rebecca to play. We built the house on a hill which already had some big trees, and I planted pecan trees and live oaks all around it. We would have more than enough shade. We put in a windmill before we built the house, and as luck would have it, we hit good sweet water, a plentiful supply of it.

Trouble comes in threes, they say. There had been Mr. Field's death and then Mrs. Clarke's. I'm not superstitious but I remembered the old expression and I wondered who would be the next to go. Except for Mr. Clarke, the people I had turned to for advice and counsel were gone and I felt strangely alone—sort of abandoned. Sally was terribly upset about her mother's death. There was no good way to comfort her, but time heals such wounds. Working on the new house and having to tend to Rebecca helped her.

All of a sudden the young girl I had married was a woman grown. The sudden pain had changed her. She laughed as she always had. That is one of the things I think of when I picture Sally—that quick low laughter. But more of the time she was serious, and she talked about going to church but, of course, the closest one was the church the Methodists had built in Santa Rita, and that was just too far off. So Sally took to reading the bible, and on Sunday she would read a passage to Rebecca and me, and she would worry about what it meant. More than once I recall her saying, "My lands, that sure don't sound like something the Lord would do." Then she would brighten up and say, "Well, this must be a mystery. It's not up to us to try to explain the Lord." After a time she stopped reading the Old Testament except for the Psalms so as to concentrate on the New Testament. She said without a preacher to explain it she would just get too confused otherwise.

She would say her prayers each night and always she ended by saying, "Lord have mercy on us poor sinners." It struck me that she looked right at me every time she said that. Well, I have heard that a man can get to heaven on his wife's coattails, in a way of speaking. I wasn't about to discourage her.

At the same time that we were putting in the windmills and dirt tanks on the two Field ranches we thinned out the herd as we had done on the other places. I had more than enough land so there was no sense in not caring for it. All of this took long days of work, but we seemed to thrive on it. They say a man can kill himself working but I never saw it happen. On the other hand I have seen quite a number of men who died from not working, for idle hands are the devil's workshop, as Sally remarks from time to time. Whiskey and hell raising are harder on your health than work by a long sight. So the hours were long and the work was hard, but we could see things that we had planned take place. There are few greater satisfactions in life.

Culley would come over every few days and have supper with us. He was on his way to being a confirmed old bachelor, though Sally nagged him to get married all the time. He would just grin and say to her that a baby sister can't go around telling her big brother what to do. Those were good days, Culley riding up on the big roan stallion that he and I had bought at Ozona for Mr. Clarke. He would sit there while I'd walk out to the gate in front of the house as he got down, and almost every time he would say the same thing. He'd say, "Tom, the sight of you is as welcome as the shadow of a rock in a weary land." Sally told me he got that from the Bible, and I reckon she ought to know.

Culley would eat with us, and we would have a drink after supper. Then he would play with Rebecca and tell her stories while Sally would settle down on the settee close to me.

Once Culley looked at me and he began to laugh. He said, "You sure as hell don't look like the Rattlesnake Kid no more. You look more like a lazy old house cat." Then he laughed at his own joke until Sally told him to hush up, and said he shouldn't talk like that in front of Rebecca.

Somehow I can't forget that particular night. Most of the things we do we never remember. For no good reason some moments stay in your mind's eye, and they are as real as when they happened. You remember things you saw and heard, the smell of the breeze, and how you felt. It was such an ordinary night. Perhaps that is its wonder.

CHAPTER 18

In the next year we gradually got all the stock branded with the Lazy E, which as you know is just an E on its back. We had good rain and a good calf crop, and I started an experiment that got me into trouble all over again with my neighbors. What happened is that I stocked Rambouillet sheep, right in with the cattle. You would have thought I had decided to go in for raising rattlesnakes and centipedes. For a fact, many an old friend cut me dead. That's the truth. They would set their mouths and turn away from me, the few times when I would come into town.

Every cattleman used to think that sheep killed out the grass and ruined the land, but I had been looking at the land owned by folks who raised sheep here and there, and I saw the same thing as with cattle. Too many will overgraze a pasture, but the right number won't hurt it. Another thing I saw, sitting one day on my horse, the sheep were eating the low grass and weeds down on the ground that cattle normally pass, and they weren't eating the taller grass and weeds that cattle favor. It struck me that not only would sheep not ruin the land, but they could graze the same land as cattle since they eat differently. At least I wanted to put it to the test.

By the end of that year I knew I was on to something good. In the spring we had sheepshearing crews come in that we paid so much a sheep for shearing, and we would give them a goat for their meals for every thousand sheep they sheared. The wool was bought by an agent who worked for a Boston company. All the wool went then, and still goes, to Boston. After the War Between the States an old blind Confederate general tried to change this. He got folks from hundreds of miles around—from as far as our county, in fact—and built a wool-processing mill on the Colorado River where Marble Falls is now. But it never made it. So Texas wool still goes to Boston to be made into cloth.

That doesn't bother me—not one whit. They pay cash money, and you don't have to sell any of your stock. This is the fascinating thing to me: you make a sale and still own the sheep. So we bought more Rambouillets, which is a breed of sheep that seems to be able to forage for itself and to do well in dry country like ours, and as time went on they had thousands of lambs. It was then that I began to do the thing that some held was downright unforgivable. I began to sell off my Herefords and build up my Rambouillets. Hell, I hate sheep. They're among the dumbest creatures God ever made. I don't like the way they smell. I can't stand to be around listening to their damned bleating and high-pitched, stuttering *ma'aa* noises. The worst thing of all about them is when you have to drive them someplace. They'll get to a little ditch and stop in dumb fear as though they were faced with the Grand Canyon, till finally one jumps over, then the others will follow. We had to train lead goats to put in with them so we could get them through gates and into pens. They seemed to have some ungovernable terror about going through any kind of gate, and I've seen grown men almost cry out of frustration trying to get them to go on through. But this is all beside the point. From a dollars-and-cents standpoint they looked like they would be very important in our part of the country. The only problem was pride. If there is one thing certain it is that the only thing a cowman can count on is his pride that he is a cowman. That may sound stupid, but it's true. There is a hell of a lot of pride in owning cows, and not much in owning sheep. But the price of cows goes up and down, but more often it goes down. We had been through good years, but with the feedlots going in up at Kansas City and a few other places, there were other ways being discovered to put weight on beef rather than to leave them out in the pastures. It was getting a little uneconomical to concentrate on range cattle where you had to have so much land to support a single cow-calf unit. Sheep ate less besides, and in bad times they had a better chance of survival in desert-like country. Hell, you just had to read your history books. The Arabs and folks like that had to settle for mutton while folks in England with lots of rain could afford to raise cattle. At any rate, that is how I saw it. Besides, it wasn't as though I was doing away with cattle. I was going to have both, and two sources of income instead of one made sense to me.

Along about that time an old man named Joe Drake from up north came down and visited with Max Hall at the bank, who sent him out to stay for a few weeks with me. Mr. Drake was a strange man, but a worker. He went out with his tools and chipped around on rocks and the like from dawn till dark. He was a geologist in the oil business and he lived in Titusville, Pennsylvania, where oil had been discovered in the 1850s. He seemed to know a great deal about his business and he sat with me one evening and said that the day would come when there would be a big demand for oil—not just as a replacement for coal oil, or kerosene, for lamps—but as a better and cheaper source of energy. He said it would do a better heating job than coal, for instance. He said he had a hunch that there was a lot of oil in the United States, and his research led him to believe that there was oil to be found in Texas. As I say, he was a peculiar duck and he was writing up an exploration journal for his company for future use. He told me that the geological formations on our ranch looked promising. He claimed that he could see the time when the Lazy E (he was talking about all our spreads) would be filled with oil derricks. I damn near ran him out of the house, except he was such a nice old man, even if he was a little on the foolish side. So all I said was that would sure as hell not happen in my day, that I wouldn't have that nasty mess on my ranch, or have a bunch of strangers wandering around in my pastures, bothering the stock, and in all likelihood leaving gates open behind them. Mr. Drake just smiled and said that times and people change, and—thinking about the sheep—and remembering my lifelong hatred of them, I had to grin and say he had a point.

I took Mr. Drake to Santa Rita, where he had hitched a ride to Fort Worth with one of our wool buyers who always traveled in style in a surrey. When he had left I felt well rid of him. He had been with me, as I say, for close onto two weeks. I had Max Hall at the bank to thank for that, for he had sicced him on me. It's always good having company when they are family or friends, but there is a tension about having a stranger around the house for an extended stay, even someone as nice as Mr. Drake. I was giving Max hell about that over at the bank and he said. "Now, Tom, don't get your dander up. Let's go over to the Main Street Bar and see if they don't have my private stock of Kentucky bourbon put back for a special occasion. The drinks will be on me." That Max was as smooth as silk. He could charm the birds out of the trees.

After a few drinks I was feeling some better and Max promised not to do me any more favors like sending Yankees out to prowl around my ranch. About that time I looked up at the mirror behind the bar and saw a slender young man come in and move to an open spot with no tables, about ten feet behind me. He was staring at my back and didn't see my eyes on him in the mirror. I turned around and looked at him. He was nervous as a cat. It looked like what I had always thought might come to pass, though I would put the idea out of my head every time it would pop up. But if things like this kept happening it would be enough to keep me out of bars, as much as I like them.

He was wearing a gun and his hand was twitching beside it. I glanced at his thin fingers and then looked up at his face.

He asked, "Tom English?"

I nodded and stood up. "Have we met?"

"I've heard some mighty bad things about you, Mr. English."

Funny that he would call me "Mr." It made me feel old. I said, "I don't know your name, and I sure don't know what you have heard about me." I began to step toward him and he glanced over his shoulder real quick, and began to back up, going five feet for every one I went toward him. When I stopped he was clear at the end of the place, a good ten paces away. Maybe thirty feet or so from me.

He said, "I've heard how you swing chairs and bottles at people."

"Well, I don't do that as a regular thing." I walked back to the bar and turned to face him. Then I said, "Who paid you to come call me out?"

He flinched ever so slightly at that and then he said, "I'm here on my own."

I thought I would try to talk some sense into him. "You can see that I don't carry a gun no more. I haven't in years. If you shoot me you'll hang for sure."

He was pale as a ghost and he said, "I never figured you for a coward, though I have heard about your pointing a gun at a poor old man, saying you were going to blow his head off, and he died of shock. That is part of what I've heard."

It was then that I knew who had hired him. Everyone had moved out of the way and I saw that no one was about to step in to give me a hand. Poor old Max was in a state. He had never carried a gun in his life. He went out the door shouting at the top of his voice, "I'm going to get the law. We'll be back in sixty seconds and you better be high-tailing it out of here by then, young fellow."

The kid looked at me and said, "Mr. English, you and I know there ain't no law in town, don't we?"

The cowboys who had been drinking in the bar slunk out of the place and I was alone except for the bartender.

"Are you going to give me a chance to borrow a six-gun or do you plan to hang for murder?"

"If you had a gun then it would be me that didn't have a chance. I like the odds better this way. I'm giving you the same chance you gave Mr. Dawson," he said.

I hadn't planned it this way. Not at the hands of a sneaky-looking kid with a twisted mouth. A feeling of disgust came over me. "Go ahead and shoot, then." He actually seemed to be having a rigor. His hand had hold of his pistol and he was standing there, shuddering. Then he yanked it out real wild like and waved it out toward me.

I said, "If you're man enough, go ahead and shoot."

The gun went off and hit the mirror behind me. He had missed by some six feet. Just then Max and some of the cowboys from the Lazy E who happened to be in town came in on the run, with their guns out. John Henderson, the bartender, came up from behind the bar with his sawed-off shotgun, and the kid dropped his pistol like he didn't have any nerves in his hands at all.

Everybody stood and looked at us and for a second I couldn't help but be sorry for him. I said, "Missing me was the luckiest thing that ever happened to you in your life. No one who hasn't experienced it can really know what it's like to be a marked man. Remember my words, boy, and don't ever wear that gun again. You nearly did a low-down thing for pay, and you would have hung for it. Besides, it don't seem to me to be a line of work that you're suited for." He didn't look like he was listening. I questioned him as to who had paid him to shoot me but he wouldn't say a word.

Then the boys took him over across the street to the jail and locked him up until Marshal Jordan or the circuit judge, Ed Wright, got to town. We didn't know when either of them would show up, but we were all agreed that this crazy kid shouldn't be wandering around loose.

I stood drinks for the house and we were there for several hours. John Henderson said, "Tom, you must have nerves of steel, demanding that the kid go ahead and shoot."

"John, since I have been drinking your whiskey for several hours to get them settled down, I will have to confess that I don't have nerves of steel. The thing is, I saw how nervous that boy was. I backed him up and then came to the bar. A six-gun, even in a shaky hand, is bad news at ten feet or less. But at over thirty feet you would be surprised how few can hit a man-sized target."

I didn't let on how badly scared I had been. It was all I could do to keep from going out to the house and strapping on my gun to go look for the Dawsons. While he hadn't admitted as much, the kid surely had been hired by them. But one thing just leads to another, and I had given my word to Sally. So I stayed and drank with the cowboys and thanked them. Max Hall and I sat down at a table and didn't leave it until we had finished that bottle of Kentucky bourbon that had been put by for him.

It was late when I got home and I was worried about what Sally would say. I needn't have for she wasn't there. She had left word that her dad wasn't feeling well, and she and Rebecca had gone over to tend to him and cheer him up. I was to come to get them the next day. I fell into the bed and slept like a rock.

CHAPTER 19

It appeared to all of us in the next few months that Mr. Sam Clarke was sinking fast. The last time I saw him the way I remembered him—strong and confident—was two weeks before he died. He had got his hands on that damn book that had come out on me. It was another one, and it was worse than the first one. It was written by a Yankee from St. Louis who had spent all of two weeks doing his "research." He never had talked to me, though later a few people in town said he had been around, asking questions. He had mostly stayed around the Taylor Hotel and talked to the people who made a practice of sitting around the lobby trading stories. You can well imagine what reliable sources of information they were. This book was called *Tom English, Millionaire Killer.* I saw on the dust jacket of the book that "this assassin is still at large."

Mr. Clarke chuckled out loud and read different stories from it to me. It had all about my killing sixteen men. It said that everyone was terrified of me as I "stalked the streets and countryside." That's a sample of its style. Then it dealt with "the insatiable greed and rapacity of the man who fenced both sides of the North Concho River, and after deadly gun battles with the lawful and traditional users of the precious, life-giving water, he unlawfully and by force of arms and terror expropriated to his own use the immense ranches of all of his neighbors. Thus has Tom English, like a robber baron in Medieval England, taken land, cattle and other property from honest, law-abiding men. Today, Tom English is one of the richest men in the entire Southwest. He stands above the law, riding roughshod over whoever is in his way."

"My Lord in heaven, Tom," Mr. Clarke laughed, "I can't imagine what I ever found to like about you." He was sitting up in his chair on the porch and he had his boots and hat on. "I'll be damned if I'll stay another day in that bed," he had said to me.

Mr. Clarke looked tired but, sick as he was, he didn't look unhappy. I couldn't bring myself to think that he wasn't going to be all right, although Doc Starret told Sally that she must prepare herself for the worst. Mr. Clarke said, "Culley tells me you're about as mean as a lazy house cat now." I laughed and said that most cats I had known were a sight meaner than I was.

Mr. Clarke was amused about most of the book except the part that said that Tom English had insinuated himself into the good graces of a senile old man, Jason Field, and got to be his heir. He said that was despicable, and that furthermore he had never known a man more in command of his faculties than Jason Field, right up to the time of his death. He sighed. "That's the way to go, like Jason did, still strong, still out riding in the pasture." He stared off the porch without seeming to notice much of anything.

Then Mr. Clarke looked at me seriously and said, "It's a shame that no one will know the things you have done for good. You were a pioneer in cross fencing and rotating your herds to save the grass. You were the first I know of out here to put in dirt tanks all over your ranches, and certainly the first in West Texas to put in windmills and water troughs in all your pastures. You put in your own hay, you found you could mix sheep with cattle, you have upgraded your Herefords and your Rambouillets. Hell, boy, I could go on and on. You have kept a big crew grubbing out the prickly pear and the mesquite to improve your land."

He shook his head. "Tell me about what you're doing with your cattle now. I don't want to hear about your damned oily sheep."

I had to laugh again. I told him about my new herd bulls. They were from the Prince Domino line and we kept them penned most of the time. We were breeding show stock and had big plans to try for the grand champion ribbon at the Fort Worth Stock Show.

Two weeks later Mr. Sam Clarke died in his sleep. Culley found him and couldn't wake him. It struck me like it was a good way to go. Culley and Sally were in a daze until well after the funeral. If anything, after this we were closer to Culley than ever. He and Sally were the sole heirs, since their sister Agnes had died with no children, and he wanted Sally and me to know all he was doing with the ranch. We told him we had absolute faith in his judgment, but he wanted to counsel with us. He began to work his place in much the same way that we did on the Lazy E. He even put in sheep, after a good bit of bellyaching. He said, "All the other ranchers got wind of how much money you're making on wool and they are buying sheep too." Culley and I thought this was funny as hell for I had been cut short by every man jack of them.

We decided to capitalize on this turn of events, so we went partners on the biggest barn you ever saw. We bought a good bit of land in Santa Rita and built the barn as a central wool warehouse. From now on we would store wool for a fee and the different buyers from Boston could come and make bids on it. Each buyer had a code book and a letter would stand for a short sentence. They kept the telegraph line hot, wiring information and getting bid authorizations. The wires they sent were nonsensical without the code books. All in all, they were a strange breed.

In a short time it looked like Santa Rita might turn into the inland wool capital of the country, and every week more buyers were showing up. It helped us put pressure on the Santa Fe for the spur from Fort Worth. We talked to the Orient Railroad folks too. The rail line would have to come before our market would be truly important. In the meantime more and more ranchers were making the decision to specialize in sheep.

Culley and I gave the town a school site in the middle of the rest of the property, and a place for a park down around the river. There were some nice things said, but to my surprise a lot of folks complained that we were planning to set up the rest of our property and make it more valuable, as though there were something wrong with that. One man turned away from me at the post office and I heard him say, like it was to himself, "The rich get richer and the poor get poorer."

In a way it hurt my feelings to find that a considerable number of people in Santa Rita hated my guts. There were people who had never met me who despised me, I learned. Sally told me, "Daddy used to say this is normal, for folks to dislike those who have more than they do."

I told Sally, "It may be normal, but it seems peculiar to me. I remember hiring on as a horse wrangler for Jason Field when all I owned was an old saddle and bridle and a good mare named Bess. I didn't despise Mr. Field. I was grateful to him." Sally said, "You're a little young to be looking back and reminiscing."

It suddenly occurred to me that I hadn't mentioned something else that I had owned: a single-action .44-caliber revolver. From the time that six-gun had first been used until now, a lot of water had gone under the bridge. The stories had grown and some were like legends. Perhaps they had been spurred on by the two books, and now there was even a song about Tom English. Culley delighted in singing it to me and listening to me cuss. He would say, "Tom, you're a terrible disappointment to blame near everyone who meets you for the first time. They have heard all the stories, and they expect to see someone about ten feet tall, not a skinny, average-sized cowboy." He would laugh and slap his leg with his hat. Can you imagine a grown man still acting like that?

I need to stop now and backtrack. I have told myself that I wasn't going to try to make myself look any better or worse than I am. I was just going to tell the truth. But I passed pretty lightly over something that worried me at the time and that has haunted me ever since. In my last talk with Mr. Clarke he asked me if I had ever been sorry about the bad things that had happened in my life. I told him, "I'm sorry about all the bad things—about all the violence. But most of it just happened, and I suppose under the same set of conditions it would happen again. Maybe if I had walked out of Malone's place that night when I was seventeen like most ordinary kids would have, the rest of the things wouldn't have happened. But the fact was, I had been frozen there; it was like I couldn't move. Afterward the other gunfights just seemed to happen."

I was covering up and he knew it. He asked, "All of them, Tom?" I knew that we were thinking of the same thing. "No sir, not all. Not when I went to get your horse, Dan." It was hard for me to talk about it, but I knew I had to face it. "I had been sent to the Circle X out on the Rio Grande to do a job and my pride got the better of my sense. I had a funny feeling at the time we followed those rustlers into Mexico. I had faced men and I had learned a simple truth. Many a man can talk about gunplay, and many can carry guns, but there are very few who can keep their heads and who are cold enough to shoot to kill when the chips are down. Even a fighter will hesitate about something like that, the taking of a human life. I had learned that I didn't hesitate, and that in a fight I saw more quickly and clearly than at any other time. I felt that I was better than other men. It was like no man or group of men could ever be quick enough to get me."

I stopped talking for a minute, for I wasn't proud of this part of my life. "I have always loved hunting. It was born in me. Going out after game is still something that is important to me. It was like that, tracking those ten men into Mexico. It seemed like fate had put me there—like Culley had shown me how to dynamite fish, and all the time he had shown me, I was thinking of the dynamite as a weapon."

I looked at Mr. Clarke. "It is the God's truth, I went down into Mexico to get Dan back out of pride so I wouldn't have to face you without him. But the thing I have trouble admitting is that I felt a tremendous joy: I was on the hunt! That shames me. I didn't see those poor hungry rustlers for what they were. I saw them not as men but as game to hunt. I stalked them and I killed them, not that they weren't showing signs of being willing to kill me. But later, as I rode Dan in a big sweep, getting out of the valley, I had to circle fairly close to their homeplace, and I heard their women crying.

"I've had bad dreams that I have told Sally about. But the dream of those women crying is one I have tried to black out of my mind, and until this moment I have never confessed it to anyone."

Mr. Clarke said, "You were young. If the same sort of thing came up again you wouldn't act in the same way."

I said, "I know I wouldn't."

I didn't want to put this in. On the other hand I wanted to tell the whole story. A man can think he knows himself and then something can happen and he finds that he didn't really know himself at all. It was six months later on a cold November day when I learned this.

CHAPTER 20

A blue norther had hit the day before. There had been sleet and a few snow flurries, and then a long dark day with a biting, cold wind and driving rain. That night the rain stopped and the wind died down. We built a big fire in the fireplace and sat close around it. Sally and I looked at the colors in the fire, listened to its occasional popping when the fire would hit a pocket of sap and a small blue or red spark would fly out, and we felt the fire's warmth as we held each other.

We had been asleep about four or five hours when I waked with a start at the sound of pounding downstairs on our front door. That, with the sound of the dogs barking, brought me out of the bed in a hurry. There is something especially frightening about unexpected, violent noises that wake you from a sound sleep in the darkness before dawn. I felt my heart pounding.

It didn't take a minute to jump into my clothes and boots and grab my Winchester. I looked out the upstairs bedroom window and could scarcely believe my eyes. Then I went down the stairs, opened the door, and ushered Jedediah Jackson into the house. It was not that he wasn't more than welcome, but that he rarely left Santa Rita. He had never been to see us before. The amazing thing was to greet the old lawyer at three or four o'clock on a black winter's morning, to look at his haggard, exhausted face.

For some reason we hadn't spoken except in greeting. I

knew he was here for a deadly serious purpose, but I could hardly bring myself to ask what it was. Sally was standing behind me, holding tight to my arm.

Mr. Jackson said, "Mrs. English, I bring terrible news. Tom, I want your word that you'll hear me out before you do anything."

I nodded at him and gestured for him to continue.

Jedediah Jackson said, "Culley Clarke is dead, shot down by a hired gunfighter."

Sally cried out. It was a strange sound, and shrill, not at all like her. We stood there, frozen by what we had heard, and then, with a long, low moan, Sally ran up the stairs to our room. I heard the door slam. I kept saying, "What? What did you say?" The fact is, I couldn't bring myself to believe it.

"Max Hall and several of your friends asked me to ride out to bring you the news. They realized how hard you would take this. Everyone knows how much Culley meant to you. The point is, he's gone, and nothing we can do will bring him back. Riders have been sent for Marshal Ben Jordan. He is said to be out in the Llano country. This is a matter for the law, and as an officer of the court, I can tell you this is how justice is to be had. I am here to ask you to let the law take its course and not to take it into your own hands."

I realized that I was crying, something I can't remember doing but once or twice since I was just a little kid. I finally got myself settled down enough to ask, "Who did it? What did he look like?"

"He's a man with no name that we have been able to find out—a strange, gaunt-looking man, dressed in black. He came into town two days ago asking for you. We could tell he was a gunfighter, with his gun tied down the way it was. He put the word out that he had come for you. He gave a youngster with a paint pony a dollar to go find you and let you know he was going to be waiting for you in Santa Rita.

"The kid went to the Lower Ranch and they told him you were here at your headquarters on the Upper Ranch. The boy was passing through the Clarke place to get here when Culley and some of his cowboys saw him and asked him where he was going. He told them his story."

Jedediah Jackson hesitated. I looked up at him and he went on. "Culley took the boy and went with him to Santa Rita. His foreman, Scott Baker, went with him. Culley went in your place. He said he didn't want you to get involved in any more trouble and that he would see if he couldn't put a stop to it."

"What happened?"

"Culley was game, dead game. He told the stranger that you had given up gunplay, and that he should move on. People who were there told me that the man in black knew about Culley, that he was your best friend. He apparently knows a lot about you. The gunfighter was heard to say, 'He might not come in if I sent for him, but he'll come if something happens to you.'

"I don't know all that was said, but it is my understanding that Culley told him that if he just had to have a fight that he could find one right there and then with him. The stranger didn't answer that, he just said, 'Draw,' and both men went for their guns. Culley died on the instant; his hand never even touched his gun."

I couldn't stop crying, though God knows I tried. I said the word, "Culley . . ." Then I said, "Excuse me a minute, Judge." Many of us called the old lawyer "Judge," though he had never served as one. With his being older, though, it was the first time I had ever said it to his face. I had to go upstairs to get myself under control, and I needed to comfort Sally.

When I got to the room she was in the bed, sobbing and crying, with her face forced down in the pillow so she wouldn't wake Rebecca in the next room. I held her and she sat up and put her head on my chest. She said, "Not Culley—not Culley." Then she asked, in such a puzzled tone, "Why? Why?" I suppose it is the question that is always asked at such times.

Sally turned to me and said, "Please don't go after him, Tom. I couldn't stand it if something happened to you."

My eyes were dry now. I felt a pounding in my ears, and my damned old mouth was twitching, like it used to do. The blood seemed to fill my head and I wanted to scream and to rage, but I didn't. I could hear my voice. It sounded so much calmer than I really was. I said, "But, Sally, you know I have to go."

She sat on the bed and wept while I unpacked Jason Field's .45. God, it felt good in my hand! But I was trembling. Fear? Rage? I buckled on the gun belt and tied down the scabbard. Then I loaded the six-gun and filled all the cartridge loops on the belt.

It was useless trying to talk to Sally. I couldn't bring myself to explain and she couldn't listen.

I went downstairs and out to the bunkhouse, where I waked up Santiago, Benito's son, and sent him to the horse trap to bring in our remuda. At night we just kept in one horse, or rather a mare, to use for this purpose before dawn. Naturally the boys called her "the night mare." This was Santiago's job. He was good at it. He had those horses figured. It was as if they played a game with him, hiding down by the river among the big pecan trees, or being at the other end of the pasture, out in the mesquite thickets. Then, when they had stopped running in circles—in their freshness and high spirits—and decided to go along with him, they would come running toward the corral, manes and tails flying, devil take the hindmost, like it was some kind of race.

Sally fixed me toast and coffee, which was all I wanted. There were surges, like excitement going through my stomach. This is when you're alive. You can be placid and feeling middle-aged, riding along in the sun in the pasture, when suddenly there is the quick buzz of a rattlesnake's tail, and on the instant something shoots through you at the same time that your horse rears up, or bucks, or jumps and shies off to the side. This is when you know you're young—you're young and completely alive—you're not dead.

I asked Sally to make sure Mr. Jackson rested before he started back to town. He stood there and his eyes looked awful tired and sad. He said, "Don't do this thing, Tom." But I had to. He knew that. Jedediah Jackson turned and went back into the house. Sally began to cry again, and I got on Joe, my favorite young horse, the one by Dan out of Bess.

Joe headed south in a lope to get me over the hills and away from the house. Then he settled into a smooth, ground-eating trot, a lot like Dan's.

The sun was coming up when I got to the fence between the Upper Ranch and the Clarke ranch. I got off to open the gate and then decided I had better limber up. I had a box of cartridges in my saddlebag and the trouble in town would damn sure be waiting for me whenever I got there. I tied Joe a good piece off. He wasn't like Bess about gunfire. Joe had always been skittish, and I decided that I would have to break him of it. Then, for the first time a sobering thought hit me. If I was still around after today I planned to break him of it.

I hadn't kissed Sally goodbye. I hadn't seen Rebecca. Hell, this was no way to think.

First I worked on smoothness and accuracy. Then I gradually went faster. Once, as a kid, I had seen a circus. A juggler had kept six plates in the air at one time. It was miraculous. I went back home and tried it with three plates, and broke them all. I got a good licking for that from my grandma. But the idea of that juggler stayed with me. I *knew* that with enough practice I could learn to do it. It was that way with the guns. I doubted very much if there was anyone alive who had fired as many thousands of rounds, or had practiced his draw as many thousands of times. I had worn out two gun belts and six scabbards through the years. Yet what I had heard of this man in black made me realize I was facing someone from a long way off. One of the "born" gunfighters. There have been just three or four of them that I have ever heard of. There is no way to practice and learn to do what they can do by nature. I was good. But I had gotten there by sheer hard work. Well, we would just have to play the hand out. The cards were dealt.

I went to untie Joe and he tiptoed all over the place like a fresh-broke colt. I finally got on him and rode over to the gate. It gave me some satisfaction to see that my bullets had almost chewed the gatepost in two. A good grouping, and from twenty feet at different speeds.

The day was gray and overcast and the north wind behind me was cool but not cold, not anything like the way it had been the day before. Texas weather is peculiar. It's impossible to predict. Although I couldn't see the sun, when I got to the Lower Ranch I figured it was a little after noon, so I ate some dried beef jerkey and drank some water from the small canteen I had on my saddle.

The land was desolate, some would say. It was semidesert

country. But to me it was beautiful. Real desolation was further west, or inside my head. The heartache at the loss of Culley Clarke was more than I could bear. I seemed to hear his voice, his laugh. The pain was physical. I felt a terrible twisting in my stomach and doubled over in the saddle. Finally I was able to straighten up. I would get that black-clothed, blackhearted son of a bitch!

The last six miles I tried to make a plan, but some things can't really be thought out all the way. I figured I'd rather be riding, tired and stiff as I was, and knowing about when I would get to Santa Rita than to be the man waiting there for me, wondering when and if I might show up. He would have heard enough tales about me that he might have help along; I would have to watch out for that.

Then the thought hit me right between the eyes. Of course! How could I have been so Goddamned stupid! Earl and Billy Dawson were sure to be there. They were the ones who had hired him. They would be there to see him take me. It stood to reason. And if he failed, they would be there to back-shoot me.

I tried to put myself into their minds. If I were Billy Dawson I might be outside with the crowd. But Earl was cautious. He was the older brother and Billy would do what Earl said. Earl would be out of sight. Where? Only one good place—the hotel. It had three stories and was the tallest building in town. Since the Taylor was the only hotel in Santa Rita you just said, "the hotel" and everyone knew what you meant. "Downtown" consisted of the hotel, the bank, the livery stable, the post office and the telegraph office, which were both in the same building, the Methodist church, three bars, and a house for fancy ladies. There were a few other one-story frame buildings. There was the general store that had been enlarged in the last year, and the insurance office that Ben Jordan's son had set up. His first name escaped me. What the hell was it? I had heard he was hoping to buy some ranchland. No time to think about that.

I branched off the main trail and circled around through the brush and the rocky hills. I would come into Santa Rita from the west. Behind me were the two small pyramid-type hills that were called the twin mountains, though they weren't mountains at all. I rode in through the low rolling hills and crossed the North Concho at the ford, and rode through the scattered houses. Then I went down a side street and followed it to the livery stable. I didn't believe anyone had seen me come into town. I took off my spurs and put them in my saddlebags. A man can trip on spurs, and they make noise.

From there I went out through the horses in the corral and climbed the fence so I would be toward the back of the hotel. It wasn't far from where I was to the hotel, and I walked in the back way. I stood in the dark hall a few minutes to give my eyes a chance to adjust, for the afternoon sun had come out. It seemed strangely bright outside after the dismal, slate-gray morning.

If I had been seen by the gunfighter he would probably wait for me outside, if that's where he was. He would have picked his place for his fight and it sure wouldn't be in a crowded hotel lobby. The point is, you don't go from light to dark where a man is waiting for you with a gun. It works the other way too, of course. I would have to be slow and careful going outside.

When my eyes had adjusted I walked into the lobby and it was like a cobra had slid out of the back hall. The folks there jumped, gasped, and froze. They were jittery, that's for certain.

I knew them all, and the Dawsons weren't there. So I walked up to the room clerk, a young girl who was new in town, and I said, "Miss, would you tell me what room Earl and Billy Dawson are in," and she said, "Room 206, sir," at the same time that her boss was telling her, "Don't answer him!" Then he said to me, "We don't want no trouble here, Mr. English. The man who has been asking about you is over yonder, sitting in a chair on the porch in front of the Main Street Bar." I looked out the window and could make out a man dressed in black sitting straight in a chair in front of the saloon, all alone. No horses were hitched to the rail in front of him. Not surprising.

He was about two thirds of a block away. I looked at him through the window for several minutes trying to determine if I had ever seen him before. I decided that I hadn't.

As I went upstairs I could hear a soft babble of voices. The hotel owner, a soft-faced man named Hank Summers, had one of those high voices that carry. You would think, if you had a voice like his, that you would learn to hold it down. I heard him say, "Did you see his eyes?" He kept rattling on. He said, "Once I was camped out and a bobcat came up. Have you ever seen a wildcat's eyes when they reflect firelight? They shined just like Tom English's did just then. My God in heaven! Those pale blue eyes of his like to have poked a hole in me!"

What a fool thing to say. I walked up the stairs next to the wall. Stairs don't creak near as much close to the wall as they do in the center. I learned that as a youngster sneaking around home at night. I never knew it would come in so handy. Funny how the mind stores up thousands and thousands of tiny details. I was thinking of this, and I thought at the same time—for you can have many a thought at once—all these things you've learned and all the labor to accomplish things, all the love you carry, this can be snuffed out in a second. I was getting old. I shouldn't be thinking like that.

I concentrated on the Dawsons. Then I thought of Culley, stone-cold dead, and it made me turn to ice. I felt chilled and hard and nothing mattered now but to get at my enemies. There was a dark, bitter taste in my mouth.

Outside room 206 I decided not to try the doorknob. It could give me away. And if it was locked, as it would be with Earl inside, it would be of no use. The shock of noise with surprise would be better anyway. I raised up my boot and gave a good hard kick, right at the latch, and the door splintered and banged open.

Earl was sitting in a chair by the window with a rifle in his lap, and he came up fast, whirling toward me. As a bird hunter, I would say I gave him a sporting chance, for I shot him on the rise. My first bullet caught him in the throat and the second hit his chest as his rifle went off way to one side of me.

Billy's pistol was clearing its holster; I had been a fool to shoot twice at Earl when the first had stopped him. There was a quick explosion and Billy was blown backward like a mule had kicked him in the chest; he flew back and crashed through the second-story window. I heard the sudden, heavy impact as his body hit the street outside, and I heard the shrieks and screams from all the people. Then I walked to the window and saw the man in black with his gun out, standing in front of the saloon looking at me as I stood in the window. Billy was flat on his back and his six-gun, which had not fired, was close to his hand. Earl was on the floor beside me, facedown with his rifle under him. No one could say it hadn't been a fair fight, although as a general rule there simply ain't no such thing as a "fair" fight. One man or the other always had the edge; planned or natural or by accident, there always is an edge.

The man in black looking at me called out in the deepest voice I ever heard, "Come out, English. Come out in the street." He said no more. None of your common street-fighter talk to get his nerve up. He was as professional as a surgeon. He carefully put his six-gun in his holster and adjusted it, butt slanted out a little, and he backed up a few steps with his hands held low.

I stepped into the hall and reloaded my .45. I carefully put three new cartridges in place of the three spent ones and snapped the cylinder shut. I turned it, checked it, and holstered the weapon, just as carefully as my unknown enemy had done. Strange that we who had never seen each other, who might have been friends, who certainly had a hell of a lot more in common with each other than with just about anyone else in the whole country, should cast this to one side. In these times there is only one thing to do. I thought of Culley and the red sickness hung before me. Hadn't enough blood been shed? No, by God! Not yet.

I went down the stairs and through the lobby to the back hall, not really noticing the stunned looks of the people, and walked out the back door. The sun was getting low. What time would it be? Maybe after five in the afternoon. It didn't matter. My mouth was dry and I felt like a tiny windmill was in my stomach, pumping excitement and quickness through my veins.

I walked around the hotel to the center of the street. The man in black had been watching the front door of the hotel and he jumped when he saw me. He wouldn't be human if he wasn't just a little nervous. Hell, his two backup men were dead, he had been waiting all day. His nerves had to be wound up as tight as a watch spring. But it sure didn't show. That had been the only part of my plan, really, to make him know I was in town and make him sweat. It didn't look like my plan had done anything but get him good and ready. So much for plans.

I walked toward him and saw that he was going to wait.

He was facing me, feet spread a little, poised. No use letting him get too comfortable. I stopped at thirty feet. I knew he would close the gap to maybe fifteen or twenty. Gunfighters know what they can expect from a handgun. A shadow of a smile flitted across his face and was gone. He started toward me.

He stopped at about fifteen feet away. He looked older than I had expected. His eyes were dull; high cheekbones, good clothes, black like they said, black from head to toe, even his boots. Who had told me about that? Pete Harris! "A man in black," Pete had said. Was Pete at another window? In the name of God, concentrate on the man before you!

Our eyes locked. He didn't look at my gun hand. I didn't look at his. At the split second when his eyes narrowed (had mine narrowed too?) his hand appeared with his gun. It didn't *go* for his gun, it *appeared* with it. In far less than a second, in the barest glimmer, the merest flash of time, I faced the nightmare I had dreamed so many hundreds of times: I faced the deadly barrel of a close-in .45 aimed right at me. I saw the flash of his gun a shaved instant before I felt the jolt of Jason's pistol in my hand, but to the ear it was like a simultaneous explosion, and then I was spinning backward and down, stunned and not believing it. You never believe it will be you.

I was conscious of blackness, of a terrible red-hot pain. God help me, was I dying? What was happening? Move, damn you, Tom English, move! The bastard killed Culley!

I struggled and still my face was in the mud that the rain from the day before had made of the dusty street. Then I fought to my knees. Where was I hit? I saw my gun on the ground but I couldn't get my hand to pick it up. Right arm —right arm won't work. I picked up the six-gun with my left hand, looked instinctively to see if the muzzle was clean. It was. I was slow—so damn slow—like in a very, very bad dream.

Why wasn't he shooting? Why was he giving me this chance to get on my feet? Was he playing cat and mouse—waiting cruelly to give me time to think I had a chance before finishing me off?

Everything was blurred. I shook my head, trying to get my eyes to focus. I had gone down hard. It was, I realized, my right forearm. The force of a .45 bullet will flatten a man if it hits any part of him. It strikes with a tremendous shock. The arm was broken; nothing worse than that. Wild, hot elation hit me and I shook my head again to clear it. Then I saw him. He was lying spreadeagled on his back. His black coat was open and there was a large red stain on the black shirt in the center of his chest. His eyes and mouth were open to the sky. He was dead.

At that moment I heard hooves pounding toward me and looked down the street. What the hell! What now? Then I saw. It was Pete Harris. He pulled his horse and whipped a shot off at me, his horse reared and he stepped off it. My bloody right arm was up and the left hand with the gun was balanced on it—muscle memory from practice long ago. I squeezed off a shot, then a second shot.

Muscle memory. It's there. You can train it into your muscles for when you need it. I looked at Pete Harris, facedown in the mud, and I saw the picture of him an instant before, spinning around, hit in the shoulder—pistol still up—my second shot hitting him in the chest and flipping him over on his face in the dark, thick mud.

Screams filled the air—barbaric screams. Probably not more than twenty or thirty people were there, but they sounded like twice as many. I looked at them, lined up on both sides of the street, and all of them had their mouths open; all of their eyes looked crazed. I chose that word with care. They were blood-crazed. It must be something in us from long ago.

God help us.

CHAPTER 21

It was the year of the worst winter. It began early and stayed late. Perhaps the rest of the country suffered as we did. I couldn't say about that. All I was able to think about, besides the constant throbbing pain in my right arm, was the condition of my sheep and cattle.

It was a minor miracle but we lost only a few hundred sheep and fewer than fifty cows. Throughout the entire state, and in fact in much of the Southwest and Midwest, entire herds starved. It was a full-scale disaster and there was a great deal of national publicity about it. Our problem was getting feed out to our stock. We were lucky for we had wagons from the fence-building days, and we had barns loaded full of hay. There was no way to move the cattle and sheep, of course, and it was difficult getting wagons through the snow to them. One blizzard followed another and the snow was eight to ten inches deep. That may not sound like much to people way up North, but we weren't set up for it. Hell, we'd go for several years without a snowflake, and here we were with snow in drifts up to a horse's belly. None of us had ever seen anything like it.

We didn't realize it at the time, but we were virtually the only ranch with large quantities of hay on hand. The terrible winter was a disaster for cattlemen all over the country. By the next year the great shortage drove the price of cattle and sheep sky-high. We sold breeding stock to ranchers for hundreds of miles around, and our steers brought unbelievably high prices when they got to market. It is a peculiar thing that the year of the great blizzards, a time of heartache for most in our part of the country, brought about a bonanza for the Lazy E.

That we should profit from hardship never occurred to any of us during that terrible time. We never thought of such a thing. We were too caught up in the daily work, the backbreaking work, of loading wagons with hay and getting them out to the herds. We had men on patrol pulling cows out of drifts, and getting sheep up so they wouldn't starve to death or freeze. That is another ridiculous thing about a sheep. If it gets down with its feet higher than its body it simply cannot get up. They are the most helpless creatures God ever made.

If you have been on horseback in the bitter cold you will understand what the men went through. You lose all feeling in your ears and nose, but the worst of all is your feet. They just hang there and the pain from the cold lances through them. They don't get the circulation going as they do when you are walking. We had case after case of frostbite, and all of the boys had bad colds, and a few had pneumonia. It's a wonder we all hadn't died of it, but cowboys are a tough lot.

Doc Starret had done a good job on my arm. Both bones in my forearm had been shattered and he had operated on it, taking out pieces and splinters of bone. Then he put everything back together again. The tendons weren't hurt. He couldn't say about the nerves. There was no feeling in my right hand, and I had, for the first time in my life, a sense of deep depression that wouldn't go away. I was to wear a cast for four weeks, and after that a splint and bandages for another eight. Sally drove me to Santa Rita to see the doctor once every two weeks in the buggy. Benito and his son Santiago rode shotgun. If some sick-hearted maverick wanted to gun a cripple they would be ready for him.

I will confess to being a less than perfect patient. In point of fact, I was a very bad one. I had no use for being stove in the way I was. It affected my whole outlook on life. There was another thing. My nerves were shot to hell. The old bad dream had started, and it was one hell of a lot more realistic now, for I had actually looked into the barrel. I had faced death's handgun. I would wake up wet with sweat, and feeling as weak as a sick little scared kid. Before, when I used to have these nightmares, I would drive them out with work—work on my draw, on my aim. I would get my confidence up and it would force the fear back into a corner. But now I was a damned helpless cripple.

One morning I decided I didn't have to be helpless. I was in town at the new hardware store that had been added on to the general store and I saw what appeared to be a spit copy of Jason Field's .45 Colt revolver. I took it out of its box and it even felt the same. I made the decision right then and there. After buying it I went to the saddle shop and had a good holster made, just like the kind I had always worn, but this was for the left side. It was ready later that day, before I had to leave to go back to the ranch. My report from the doc was good, but my arm was to stay in the cast for a time. I bought a gunbelt for the new holster, laid in a stock of cartridges, and got everything boxed up and loaded in the wagon without Sally's knowing anything about it.

I went into training the next morning. Sally found out, but by this time I was so worked up that she didn't say a whole lot. I enlisted Santiago to help me. He would tie the holster with its leather thongs down on my left leg. By God, if the right arm didn't heal right, and I still had no feeling in that hand, I would have to train some new muscles in my left arm and hand.

We had a long barn about half a mile from the house where we stored wood during sheepshearing season in the spring. There were pens nearby for use at that time for holding the sheep, and also for the time when we went through the bloody business of marking lambs. But now the pens and barns were empty. It was a covered place and gave protection from the bite of the north wind.

Santiago and I would walk through the snow every morning after breakfast to the wool barn. While he built a fire inside, I would set up a target on the far wall, and get the six-gun out and load it, and set up the boxes of cartridges. Inside the empty barn the smell of wool remained. It was a smell of lanolin, of the oil that is in the wool. It made me think of the sheepshearers. A huge wool sack would be suspended and one man would be inside it. The other workers would throw in an entire fleece from a sheared sheep and he would tromp it down, working hard as more and more wool got thrown in. His boots would be soaked with the dark, greasy oil of the wool when he got out. They would be soft and supple, but I don't suppose they would ever take a good shine again.

Santiago and I would warm our feet at the fire, holding them so close that sometimes they would smoke and the sudden heat would make us cuss and jump back. Then we would stomp around, to get the circulation going. When I felt warmer and ready to go I would hold my good left hand down low to the fire and flex it to take the winter stiffness out.

Trying for speed and accuracy with my left hand was the most awkward, the most aggravating thing I have ever tried in my entire life. I found myself crying from the frustration, and I would cuss out the world and myself and Santiago, and all the while he would grin, for he knew me well. I am trying to give you some picture of the total agony of that first month of practice.

I had a fine Elgin pocket watch. Before I began practicing I would snap open the gold cover on the face of the watch and would put it down by the cartridges. My day's routine was to be ordered. I practiced exactly two hours in the morning and exactly two hours in the late afternoon. I was upset when I got a few blisters the first week, but they turned to calluses fast enough.

I suppose I was half off my head. I was jumpy as a cat, hard to get along with, and mean as sin most of the time. Thank the Good Lord that the people around me were patient and understanding. Trying to master that left-handed gun became an obsession. I even dreamed about it.

The point is, I knew I could do it. My body just wouldn't do what my mind told it to do. I could picture that six-gun leaping out of its scabbard and throwing lead on the instant, right where it was pointed. I made myself relax. I was trying too hard, gripping too hard—even clinching my teeth.

I exercised the arm and the hand. I roped left-handed, threw a knife with that hand, tried throwing washers left-handed at a hole in the ground—an old game that the cowboys used to play after supper in the summer when the day stayed light until so late.

Then it happened. All of a sudden I moved from awkwardness to ease. The grace wasn't there nor the swift sureness. But I could defend myself.

I wasn't helpless anymore!

There is a wonderful feeling when you accomplish something you have worked hard to learn. It's difficult to explain. Even if what you're doing, the goal you have set for yourself, isn't especially important in the eyes of others, if you have a goal, even a simple one, and achieve it, you have won a victory.

The nightmares stopped.

After that the gun handling and marksmanship would stay the same for a week or two. I would get discouraged until, all of a sudden, I would vault up to another plateau. There was a sweetness to me in these small victories that goes beyond words.

Sally seemed to understand. I had never told her very much about my fear, but she knew. She was with me when I would cry out in my sleep and wake up wide-eyed in the dark of night, at the time when all of us are weakest. Sally understood my fear, but she thought I should turn my back on gunplay forever. She was convinced that was my way to sanity and to survival. She would say, "Hasn't there been enough death?"

Of course there had been. There had been more than enough. Twenty men were dead. Twenty lives had been cut short by my hand, and this didn't count John Dawson. In the times when I thought of this I was sick with remorse. Then I would try to shut it from my mind.

When the day had come and I got the final splints and bandages off, I took a stiff, bent arm from the sling and painfully straightened it. Slowly I opened and closed my right hand. The huge ugly scar on my forearm was a reminder of a time I wanted to forget, and I rolled my sleeve down and buttoned it.

Spring is a time of miracles. The snow had long since melted, and our pastures had never been that green before. The slow melting of the snow had permitted the moisture to soak in deep and not run off as it would in a hard shower. It is incredible what enough water will do to this almost desert country. There were bluebonnets and Indian paintbrushes and a blanket of rich green grass. There were leaves on all the trees. In the warmth of the spring days, with constant exercise, my right hand slowly got all sense of feeling back. That which was dead became alive.

My practice now was more with the right hand. I didn't want to look like one of those crazy vaqueros of Judge Roy Bean's, so I got long loops added to my holsters, like Joe Slade had worn when I faced him in Villa Plata. This way I could wear two guns down low, but only one gun belt. I liked the feeling of balance that I got from wearing two guns. It felt natural. I would draw with one six-shooter and then the other. When I drew both it wasn't quite as quick as it should have been, but then I learned to relax and not try to get there as fast with my left as with my right. That would never happen. So the right would jump and fire, and the left would be on the target answering before the sound of the first shot died away. It was a double explosion, so close it was almost like one.

I began to spend a good deal of time with Scott Baker at the Clarke ranch. He had been the foreman under both Mr. Sam Clarke and also Culley. I knew him well and Culley had told me that Scott had forgotten more about ranching than most people would ever know. The more time I spent with him, the more I respected him.

With the deaths of Mr. and Mrs. Clarke, with the deaths of Agnes and Culley, Sally's sister and brother, we had another 180 sections in the Clarke main ranch, plus the thirty-five sections of that godforsaken but somehow beautiful ranch out on the Rio Grande, the one Mr. Clarke carried as the Circle X. He had never used his big C brand out there. He had kept the brand the former owner had used.

I had still been down with my arm after the operation when Sally talked to me about it. I remember almost crying again at the thought of the loss of Culley. "Hell, we have more land than we know what to do with now," I had said. But Sally reminded me that Culley had intended all along that everything he owned would someday be for Rebecca. It would just be added to what we had; all of this was for a very sweet little girl who didn't have a worry in her head. Her world right then was full, for our cat had five new tiny kittens, eyes still closed, and Rebecca would lie beside them by the hour, while the mama cat licked and bathed her babies.

It made my head spin when I put it down on paper.

Lazy E Ranch	10 sections
Harris Ranch	75 sections
Dawson Ranch	90 sections
Field Upper and Lower Ranches	206 sections
Clarke Main Ranch	180 sections
Clarke Circle X Ranch	35 sections
	596 sections

The Lazy E brand was going on all the stock on the adjoining Clarke ranch. I left the Circle X brand for the distant ranch above Langtry. I didn't know if we should keep that place or not. We would worry about that later. But right now we had 596 sections. That is to say, 596 square miles! To look at it another way, a section is 640 acres, so we had 381,440 acres. A man could ride for months and not cover all of it.

I had made Scott Baker our head honcho. He looked after the whole shebang on a day-to-day basis. He had made Jim Farr foreman on the Clarke ranch and we sent Joe Burnett out to head up the Circle X and get it fenced. It was just a hunch, but with the unlimited water in the Rio Grande, if we could find a way to pump it we might turn that ranch into a showplace. What with Santa Rita growing the way it was—there must be five hundred people there by now—it would be good to get clear away from all the confusion every now and then. I liked the idea of having a kind of sanctuary. The more I thought about it the more I thought we might just keep the Circle X.

Marshal Ben Jordan was getting on in years and allowed that he was tired of traveling his circuit. With Santa Rita expanding by leaps and bounds the few men who made things happen there, like Max Hall and Jedediah Jackson and Lewis Westbrook (who had put in the new hardware store next to his general store), talked him into hiring on as sheriff of Tom Green County. Of course Tom Green County was state-sized in those days by Eastern standards. That was before they carved other counties out of it. When the marshal fussed and worried about this they said, "We'll even let you hire two deputies to do the traveling part," and he brightened up considerably. The idea was for him to keep the peace right there in Santa Rita. Marshal Jordan hired two ornery old Texas Rangers who were ready to settle down. One of the deputies worked out of Villa Plata and the other out of Sherwood. It made all of us breathe easier having them around. We felt like we could look forward to having law and order.

Along about this time we had a barbecue to celebrate the Fourth of July. We set up for it at the Lower Ranch, close to Santa Rita. Folks came from a hundred miles around. The boys had dug trenches and put iron bars over the fires in them and were barbecuing a dozen full sides of beef. There were enough potato salad and frijoles, son-of-a-bitch stew, tamales and tortillas for an army. Naturally we had kegs of beer and a fair number of bottles of bourbon and tequila, and many a bottle of mezcal, a Mexican drink that I never cared that much for. For one thing, most mezcal bottles have a fat worm in them from the maguey cactus plant that they use to make the liquor. Worms have their place in the scheme of the Lord's creation, I reckon, but it don't seem to me that they should be in a bottle that I'm drinking from.

After we had eaten, as the afternoon wore on, the cowboys took some metal plates, the kind we always carried in our chuck wagons, and they nailed one of them to a tree. They were having a high time as they went about setting up their contest. One man put his back to the tree that had the plate nailed to it and he stepped off seven paces, maybe twenty feet or thereabouts. Then he drew a line in the dirt. Each man who wanted to enter put down a silver dollar on an empty beer keg. Although there must have been close to two hundred people at the barbecue, most of them men, there were only about twenty who put up money to enter. After all, a cowboy earned a dollar a day and his keep, so that was a fair-sized bet. The idea was that the man who got the most shots into a plate inside of ten seconds would win the money.

The first man was drunk as a hoot owl, and he missed all six shots. The second held his pistol with both hands, closed one eye, stuck out his tongue a little from the side of his mouth, and had one hit out of four shots when time was called on him. It went like that. The marshal, our new sheriff, and his two deputies, didn't enter, but they set themselves up as judges. They were also going to make sure that no fights broke out that day. When some men drink they get happy but, as everyone knows, there are those who turn ugly. That hot, sunny Fourth of July, though, there was not a sign of trouble.

When it was all done Santiago had won. He had four hits and had gotten all six shots off under the time limit. He was bowing and waving his hat around and acting the good-natured fool when he made a suggestion. He said,

"Let's try to talk Mr. English into giving us a show." They all took it up and I was grinning and saying, "Hell no," while those cowboys were all around me, egging me on. I suppose it was because I'd had a few drinks that I agreed. There was another reason that began to take form as well. Anyway, I agreed. I asked Santiago to put three new tin plates up on the target tree, one on top of the other in a line, and I walked up the hill from the river to the house to get my guns, for I never wore them now. One gun tied down is an invitation. Two looks like you're out hunting trouble.

When I came out of the house and walked down the hill with both guns on, both tied down, there was a hush, and then a lot of excitement. I took a drink, and then checked each gun. The sun was low in the west and the heat of the day was dying down. There was no wind. The people, all two hundred of them, were quiet. They stood in a big half moon behind me.

I took my position at the line drawn in the ground and felt a surge of excitement as my right gun seemed to leap out of its holster. I didn't rush it. I really felt I was taking my time for I wanted to get the bullets in a tight pattern. In a shade under five seconds all six had chewed out a hole in the dead center of the top plate.

The people began to holler and cheer, but stopped as I put away the right gun. The left jumped out and I pushed myself for good time. The first shot was high on the plate but the others were well grouped in the middle.

Well, you talk about hell raising! Those cowboys were all over the place until Santiago stood on the keg and waved his arms to get them to calm down. By this time I had both six-guns reloaded.

The people didn't know exactly what to expect, and they were all looking at me and at the third plate. I hesitated a few seconds and then went for both guns. The right was up and firing before the left was leveled on the target, but it was a right close thing, and the sound of both guns firing together was like you would imagine a cannonade might be. First the right, and at the instant of its explosion, the left, one after another, until all twelve cartridges had blasted out one long, percussive roar. Shock-wave echoes drifted over us; we stood, ears ringing, the people stunned—in total silence. The last light of sunset cast a blood-red glow, an unreal shade of orange and red, on the trees and the men, and it showed a huge hole in the center of the third plate that had been hit twelve times. Then all hell broke loose. First old Benito gave me a great bear hug and stood back, with a broad grin on his face. Then Max Hall was pounding me on the back like an idiot, saying, "That was without a doubt the most incredible, the most awesome sight I have ever seen in my born life!"

Later Marshal, or, rather, Sheriff Jordan said, "Tom, you may have been drinking a little, but you hadn't been drinking that much. You couldn't have been and pulled that stunt. I'm going to have to agree with Max that I have never seen anything like it before, and I know I never will again. But, Tom, I'm a little puzzled. You're the last man to show off—and God knows your reputation was already made. What made you do it?"

We were on a bench, off at one side, and the men, still excited, were gathering up their things so they could leave. I answered, "It is a little hard to say. I guess I wanted to show off a little. The drink had loosened me up. To be honest, I've been tied in knots since that last fracas. When I got to the house and was putting on the guns I thought I should back out. I don't have anything to prove, and if I did poorly the word might get out. Hell, it was sure to get out. But as you may know, I've been working hard with my guns; I was confident I would do all right."

I took off my hat and tried to look into my real reasons. Then I continued, "I decided that with this crowd it would be an opportunity to let the word get around that I wasn't crippled up, that I wasn't helpless. I wouldn't want to have to shoot any more young kids who might figure on taking me."

Sheriff Jordan rolled another cigarette and we sat there in the twilight as the people left. Finally he said, "The story of what happened here will spread like wildfire. You know how people talk. The truth will be stretched and in six months time it staggers the imagination to try to think of the tale that will be told. You couldn't have planned and staged this any better. There are people here from at least a hundred miles around. I believe you accomplished your purpose."

He said, "The time is coming to this part of the state when gunplay will be over."

I remember saying, "I pray to God it does soon."

I asked him if they had ever found out who the man in black was. He said they never had and probably never would. There had been reports of him in the sheep and cattle wars in New Mexico. Some had reported that he had been in Tombstone, Arizona, before that. Others had heard stories of him in Dodge City, Kansas. He had been a drifter, a killer, a paid gun. We would never know more.

Sheriff Jordan said, in his low voice, "You've been lucky." I remember answering, "I know it. But there are different kinds of luck. I have spent my adult life trying to get that edge that can spell the difference between life and death. You know that out of a thousand men who carry a gun, not more than one or two will kill without hesitation. That is one edge I forced myself to have. Jason Field drilled this necessity into me. But it was more than that. I think of luck this way: it's *when preparation meets a challenge.*" I bore down on those last words to make my point. "That is why I have put in so many thousands of hours in practice. Because of my past I was certain that I would face a challenge. When preparation meets this challenge people often call the outcome 'luck.' But the edge, the advantage I have, has been the biggest part of it."

Sheriff Jordan rose to go. He shook my hand and put his left on my shoulder. He left me with these words, "Let's hope you never need to use that edge again."

I walked up to the house, tired from the day. Sally was on the porch and I sat down beside her.

"Do the guns come off now?"

"Yes, Sally, they do. I hope they won't be needed again. There is work to be done on the ranch, a lot of work."

We were quiet together, the way people long married can be. It wasn't strained. It was a good moment. Her hand touched my arm and I knew what she was trying to tell me. I put my hand over hers.

"Sally, I would like to accomplish something worthwhile. I would like to be remembered as something other than the meanest man in West Texas."

About the Author

H. B. Broome's great-grandfather was the U.S. marshal in that part of West Texas which is the setting for this book. The family ranch was located at Broome, Texas—named after the author's grandfather, the first man to head the Texas and Southwestern Cattlemens Association as well as the Texas Sheep and Goat Raisers Association. H. B. Broome now lives in Arlington, Texas.

TILLAMOOK COUNTY LIBRARY
210 Ivy
Tillamook, Oregon
842-4792

1. Borrowers are responsible for books drawn on their card.
2. Fine-5¢ a day for overdue books.
3. Scotch tape use, other iniury to books and losses must be made good to Library's satisfaction.